The Reunion

Charles L Freeman Jr

Cover Art by Jonathan Marcial

Printed in the United States of America

First Edition: November 2013

To book Charles L. Freeman, Jr., contact Terry Mitchell Collier of 20 Mill, Inc @ tamcollier@gmail.com.

ISBN-10: 061589206X
ISBN-13: 9780615892061

*Dedicated to Maurice White and
Earth, Wind & Fire
Thank you for over four decades of musical excellence*

Prologue

Music industry executive Lorenzo (Chocks) Taylor awoke drenched in sweat at 4:30 in the morning. Darkness engulfed the master bedroom suite of his palatial, tri-level Hollywood Hills home; his neighborhood of winding streets and secluded houses hidden behind high gates and walls was quiet in the hours before dawn in Los Angeles. He sat upright in bed, listening to the silence, his mind racing with thoughts of where his life might be headed in the next few weeks.

It was mid-August 2013 and during the coming weekend, he'd be attending his 20-year high school reunion in San Diego, California, an event that Lorenzo was eyeing with a combination of excitement and dread. The former because he'd be seeing his old crew, four guys that he'd known practically all his life and who called him Chocks because of his childhood love of the vitamins of the same name, and the latter because Lorenzo realized that this milestone put him just two short years away from the Big 4-0. He'd tried to find out if his old girlfriend, Tina Davis, was attending but so far, her name wasn't on the list of those who'd registered. Then there was tonight.

For the first time in ten years, Lorenzo was looking for a new job. It wasn't that he **wanted** a new job per se; generally speaking, he was happy with his current one. And under normal circumstances, he wouldn't think of leaving the company where he'd spent the past ten years of his very successful career. A career that had brought Lorenzo a long, long way from his days as a struggling free-lance songwriter/producer.

But circumstances were no longer normal at Wilshire Records a year after the company's sale to a Japanese conglomerate. Lorenzo, used to doing pretty much whatever he wanted when it came to getting his artists' projects completed, was growing increasingly frustrated with the monetary restrictions imposed by the new owners. And if the rumors he was hearing about even more cost-cutting measures once the current company-wide review was finally finished were true, things were probably going to get worse before they got better.

Three months ago, when he'd asked his lawyer, Phillip Walker, to discreetly look around and see if there were any available jobs at other record companies that he might consider pursuing, Lorenzo figured nothing would really interest him. He knew that positions for a senior level executive with his track record were far and few between and seldom came open, especially not on the West Coast. Plus, he wanted to spend more time in the studio, producing tracks for at least two-three artists a year, and that might be a deal breaker for many companies.

So, when Phillip called three days ago and said that Sylvia Andrews, the beautiful and ruthlessly ambitious president of Montclair Records, the top label in the business for the past five years, wanted to meet with him, Lorenzo was intrigued. Known as a sharp executive, Andrews had the reputation of being a fierce competitor and ruthless operator who felt right at home among her male counterparts in the rough and tumble world of the music business. While he'd never worked with her, Lorenzo had met Sylvia at several events such as awards shows and other music industry functions and admired her accomplishments. The only real drawback was that even though Montclair had an office in LA, their headquarters was in New York and Lorenzo had no real desire to move there.

As he stripped the sweat-soaked sheets and pillowcases from his bed, Lorenzo thought about the meeting he and Phillip were scheduled to have that evening with Sylvia. He figured that she must have something in mind, even though he or Phillip hadn't been able to find out exactly what it might be. But they were both convinced that she did because Sylvia Andrews wasn't known as someone who wasted her valuable time having a meeting just to have one.

Unable to fall back asleep as dawn approached, Lorenzo decided to go for a run around near-by Lake Hollywood. As the sun came up over the city that had been home to him for the past fifteen years, he ran and listened to old-school R&B on his iPhone. Exercise always put

Lorenzo in a good frame of mind and after logging three miles on the circuitous path around the lake, it was with a much clearer head that he walked home.

As he soaked in his Jacuzzi tub and watched Sports Center on the flat-screen TV mounted on the wall in front of him, Lorenzo was hit with a sudden, electric thought: *what would he do if Sylvia Andrews actually offered him a job tonight?*

Chapter 1

Thursday Night

Tim's, a Los Angeles restaurant and wine bar located on a non-descript stretch of Pico Boulevard of auto body shops, liquor stores and a hodgepodge of storefront shops that was being transformed by an influx of restaurants, shops and art galleries on the city's ever-changing Westside, was the last place anyone would expect a high-level business meeting to take place. That was one reason why Lorenzo had selected it for tonight's dinner meeting. The other, and most important one, was that as a silent partner in the place, he knew that Tim Barnes, whose name was on the front door and business license, would ensure that the meeting stayed private. Even though he was currently working without a contract while the label's new owners were finishing up a company-wide review, Lorenzo didn't want or need anyone from his employer, Wilshire Records, where he was Vice-President of Artists & Repertoire, to know that he and his attorney were meeting with Sylvia Andrews. This was an appointment that didn't appear anywhere on his calendar, not even the one on his phone.

Six foot, two inches tall and blessed with smooth medium-chocolate skin, Lorenzo carried 185 pounds of well-toned muscle on his frame thanks to thrice-weekly workouts with a personal trainer and daily sessions on the treadmill at home. He liked to dress well as he not only had good taste and an eye for fashion, but possessed the financial means to indulge both. Having come straight from work, he was wearing his version of business casual: a royal blue J. Moseley

Bespoke suit, light-blue checked dress shirt with monogrammed French cuffs and no tie and Cole Haan suede loafers. Unlike many of his industry peers, Lorenzo had no piercings or tattoos and didn't wear the usual jewel-encrusted Rolex on his left wrist. He opted instead for a platinum Tag Heuer that matched his custom-made Treble Clef symbol cufflinks.

After getting his claim ticket from the parking valet, Lorenzo pulled the front door open and entered the restaurant. The bar area to the right of the hostess stand was packed and noisy, without an empty table in the room or stool at the bar itself. Tim Barnes was helping the bartender fill drink orders and waved to Lorenzo when he saw him come in. Lorenzo smiled at the hostess who said, "Good evening Mr. Taylor, Tim told me you'd be in tonight."

"Hi Jessica. It looks like you've got a great crowd for a Thursday," Lorenzo said as he waited for Tim.

"Yes, we do. It's been like this every night lately," Jessica said as she grabbed four menus and walked over to a group standing near the door. "Parker, your table is ready. Please follow me."

Two well-dressed couples followed Jessica to their table as Tim came from behind the bar and greeted Lorenzo with a big smile and half-hug. "Jessica says it's been like this all week," Lorenzo said with a bit of disbelief in his voice as he looked around again. "Why didn't you tell me when we talked yesterday?"

Tim smiled. "I wanted you to see it for yourself. The new menu has made a difference and that positive review in 'Let's Eat LA' certainly helped too." Tim paused. "Getting a full liquor license would make an even bigger difference."

Based on their previous conversations about hiring Tim's brother, a land-use consultant who knew his way around the corridors of City Hall, to secure a full-liquor license for the restaurant, Lorenzo knew the response Tim was hoping for. "Not a penny over 10Gs and tell Dante half now, the other half when the license comes through."

Tim nodded. "I'll get him on it right away. I'll use the City National account."

Lorenzo nodded and changed the subject back to the reason he was there tonight. "Is everything good to go?"

"Phillip's already at the table and Anita will be your server," Tim said.

Lorenzo nodded. "Good. Make sure you bring Sylvia to the table personally."

Tim smiled. "Not to worry. I got the photo you sent over and Jessica knows who to look for." Lorenzo wasn't leaving anything to chance tonight.

Phillip Walker, dressed in a medium-gray chalk pinstripe suit, white dress shirt with French cuffs and burgundy tie with white pin dots and seated facing the doorway in the last booth in the room, was talking on his cell phone when Lorenzo slid into the seat across from him. "I'll be home in a couple of hours," Phillip said as he shook hands with Lorenzo across the table. "No, I'm having dinner with a client. I'll call you when I leave here." He listened as Anita walked up to the table carrying a tray with an iced drink in a tall glass. "Love you too baby." Phillip ended the call and placed his phone on the table. Anita placed the glass in front of Lorenzo and said, "Good evening Mr. Taylor. One Arnold Palmer as usual."

Lorenzo smiled at his favorite server. "Good evening to you too Anita. Thanks. There's going to be three of us tonight."

Anita nodded and said, "Tim briefed me. I'll be back when your guest arrives." She turned and walked away.

Lorenzo sipped his drink before speaking to Phillip. "Checking in with the wife I see." He shook his head and chuckled. "Man, you married guys are on a short leash."

Phillip laughed as he sipped his Chardonnay. "Spoken like a true bachelor. Take it from me – a happy wife means a happy life for yours truly."

"Does your 'happy wife' know you're screwing your secretary?" Lorenzo said with a slight smirk on his face.

Phillip ignored Lorenzo's question and smoothly changed the subject. "So, let's talk before Sylvia gets here."

"I'm listening."

"We know she's looking for a new senior VP for their urban division and you're her number one draft pick. Let's play it cool and not commit to anything she says."

"Do you know who else she's talked to?" Lorenzo asked.

Shaking his head slightly, Phillip said "No, but I'm fairly sure it's a short list. Very few people out there on your level not under contract right now. You're one of the few true free agents these days." Phillip looked past Lorenzo and saw Tim leading a beautiful woman to their table. There was also a large man wearing a black suit, white shirt and black tie trailing them who appeared to be some sort of security person. Phillip tilted his head towards Lorenzo and said, "She's here."

They both stood to greet Sylvia Andrews. Lorenzo nodded at Tim who nodded back and turned to walk away. The other man moved to sit at a table where he could see both the doorway and their table.

Standing 5'10 with shoulder-length hair and carrying about 145 well-proportioned pounds on her yoga-toned frame, Sylvia was a former Xerox corporate manager who got into the music industry almost two decades ago. She was personally recruited by the legendary Saul Hudson, the then-chairman of Montclair Records who she impressed at a Harvard alumni dinner in New York City with her ideas for marketing to a constantly evolving consumer base. She was dressed in a knee-length emerald green dress and nude-colored peep-toe Christian Louboutin platform pumps with 5-inch heels and carried a yellow Birkin leather bag. Sylvia offered a well-manicured hand in greeting to both men and everyone said hello. As she sat down in the seat that Lorenzo had been in, Phillip and then Lorenzo slid into the one across from her.

"I appreciate your picking a place where we can have privacy," Sylvia said.

It was Phillip who smiled and responded. "Well, you know what they say about discretion being the better part of valor."

Sylvia smiled in return. "Indeed it is."

Lorenzo raised his left hand to get Anita's attention who came over carrying three menus which she handed to each of them.

"Good evening. My name is Anita and I'll be your server tonight." She looked at Sylvia. "May I bring you a drink?"

"Bring me a glass of your best merlot." Sylvia gestured over her right shoulder to where her security man sat stoically with his eyes constantly moving to take in the entire room. "And make sure you get his order too."

"Right away. Our specials are on the right side of the menu; the catfish is especially good tonight. Would you like an appetizer to get started?"

"Thank you Anita. Give us a couple of minutes," Lorenzo said.

Anita smiled and said, "Certainly." She looked at Sylvia and said, "I'll be right back with your wine" before turning and walking over to the bodyguard's table to take his order.

"You eat here often, don't you Lorenzo?" Sylvia said. "What do you recommend?"

Lorenzo and Phillip exchanged a glance with Lorenzo slightly raising his eyebrow. He turned back to her. "I've eaten here a few times and I've never been disappointed. The stuffed filet rib eye steak would go well with the wine you selected."

"Well, in that case, I'll let you order it along with a house salad for me," Sylvia said as she closed her menu and placed it on the table next to her Samsung Galaxy S4 phone. She smiled knowingly at Lorenzo whose mind was racing as he tried to figure out how much she knew about his connection to the place.

Phillip closed his menu and put it on the table. "I think I'm going to have the catfish special."

Anita arrived with Sylvia's wine which she placed in front of her. "Are you ready to order?"

Lorenzo looked up. "Yes we are."

※❈※

Honolulu International Airport

A tall, curvy, long-legged woman with medium chocolate skin and shoulder length black hair, dressed in a multi-colored print sundress and wedge slides, pulled a small carry-on bag behind her as she walked to the check-in islands in the Hawaiian Airlines terminal. Upon arriving at the check-in area, she showed her boarding pass and headed down the jet-way to the plane. When she reached the door of the aircraft, the flight attendant directed her to a Business Class seat. She stowed her carry-on in the overhead bin and settled into her window seat and fastened her seat belt. Taking a deep breath and then exhaling, she bowed her head, said a brief prayer, crossed herself and opened her eyes as a flight attendant finished giving pre-flight instructions. The plane, crowded with noisy tourists returning to the mainland, pushed back from the gate and started its roll on the tarmac. Flight #3014 from Honolulu to San Diego was about to start its long journey across the Pacific Ocean.

Tina Davis was going home.

Chapter 2

"So, that's it in a nutshell," Sylvia said as she sipped her coffee. "Lorenzo, you're the best at what you do and I want you at Montclair Records. No disrespect to Josh; he's been a great record man his whole career. No one has been better over the last 40 years; I give him that. But times and the business have changed and continue to change. You deserve to be with a company that's prepared to evolve with the new music and technology. And frankly, I just don't think Wilshire is that company anymore. If it was, you wouldn't have been working without a contract for the last three months and Phillip wouldn't have responded so favorably when our search firm contacted him about you." Sylvia paused and looked at Phillip who nodded slightly. "Montclair is where your talents can best be used. And yes Lorenzo, that includes your spending more time in the studio," she said with a confident smile.

Lorenzo calmly sipped from his drink as Phillip leaned forward and looked directly at Sylvia. They'd agreed that he'd just listen and Phillip would do all the talking for now. But he did like what Sylvia said, especially the part about his spending more time in the studio. If Lorenzo had one real complaint about his current job, it would be that he didn't get to produce as many artists as he once did.

Phillip was direct and to the point. "When can we expect to see an offer in writing?"

Now it was Sylvia's turn to be blunt and she turned to Lorenzo. "Does this mean you're interested?" She'd had her people do a full vetting on him and she knew he was itching to spend more time in the studio. Sylvia knew she'd gotten Lorenzo's attention by bringing that up.

"You could say that," Lorenzo replied with little emotion in his voice.

Sylvia liked his response so she pushed forward. "Do you have any questions for me?"

Phillip nodded and Lorenzo shifted his weight in the booth before he spoke.

"Just a couple. I've taken a look at your current artist roster and in order to make a decision, I'd need some information on their contract status in terms of length and albums owed."

Sylvia was impressed. She wasn't the only one who'd done their homework. "I think something could be arranged as long as you agree to keep that information confidential," she said.

"Of course," Lorenzo said before continuing. "If I took this job and at this point, I want to make it very clear that it's a big 'if', 1) who would I report to, 2) if I'm spending time in the studio, who's going to have my back in the office, 3) besides any new acts I signed, who on the current roster would I be able to produce, 4) what are your production budgets and 5) is there any chance of me staying in LA and working out of your office here?"

Sylvia's people had done their research well. They'd told her that Lorenzo would be interested, but wouldn't jump at the first offer of a job in New York City. He was a Californian through and through who loved living and working in Los Angeles.

"Well, of course, you'd report to me directly, but at Montclair, we take the team approach to the music we release. You'd primarily over-see A&R and promotion, but marketing, sales, digital media, video and publicity all have input before we put anything out. Sure, you could spend time here each month, but your base would be in New York. I like having my team near me."

Lorenzo waited a moment before responding. "Define 'input' if you don't mind."

"What that means is that we look at all aspects before we release any product," Sylvia coolly replied. "I can't tell you more than that unless you're working for me. But as you can see by our market share over the last five years, we know what we're doing. You can produce anyone on the roster as long as everyone feels comfortable with the songs and direction of the project, production budgets are negotiable to a point depending on the artist contract, and as far as the office, you can bring in anyone you want as your second-in-command." She looked at her watch. "I've got a plane to catch. Can you ask the waitress to bring the check please?"

Lorenzo said, "This one is on me."

Sylvia gathered her phone and bag. "Thank you. I'll take you to my secret meeting place the next time you're in New York. Now, unless you have more questions, I'll call Jeffrey Weinberg and tell him to get started on an offer sheet." Weinberg headed up business affairs at Montclair. "I'm sure we can have something to you by close of business tomorrow at the latest. That way, you can review it over the weekend and respond on Monday." Sylvia didn't believe in long, drawn-out negotiations and wanted to wrap this one up as quickly as possible.

"Jeffrey has my cell number," Phillip interjected. "Tell him he can call me tonight if he wants to."

"I'll pass that along." Sylvia turned to Lorenzo. "Lorenzo, I hope that this is the start of a great business and personal relationship. I've admired your work from afar and I'd love to have the opportunity to work together."

Lorenzo paused as he decided whether or not to ask one last question. What the hell he figured. This might be the only time he'd have the chance to find out.

"Who else are you talking to?"

Sylvia didn't hesitate. "Ken Williams and Lewis Purcell, but you're the one I want."

9

"Why is that? They're both very talented and experienced people." Lorenzo had to know.

"They don't know music like you do," Sylvia said. "Oh sure, they're both good at what they do, but they can't do what you do in the studio." She knew that would appeal to his ego.

Lorenzo smiled as they all stood and Sylvia extended her hand to Lorenzo who shook it and then to Phillip who did the same. "It's been a real pleasure meeting with you this evening."

Lorenzo spoke for them both. "As it's been for us as well."

Sylvia smiled too. "I hope you'll like the offer Lorenzo. I really want you on my team." She turned to Phillip. "I'll make sure Jeffrey reaches out to you as soon as possible."

Sylvia turned and followed her security man out the front door where a waiting black Escalade idled at the curb. Lorenzo and Phillip watched through the window as the man opened the rear passenger door for Sylvia. She entered the SUV, he closed the door and got into the front passenger seat and the vehicle pulled out into traffic. It was Lorenzo who spoke first. "You think she's serious?"

"We'll know when we see something in writing."

Lorenzo nodded his head. "You're right. But, I'm sure Josh will match the offer."

Phillip shook his head. "Read my lips; Tokyo will never let that happen. You know it and I know it."

The men stood and walked towards the front of the restaurant as a man discreetly watched them from a seat at the bar. Lorenzo said, "That's where you're wrong Phil. Josh doesn't want to lose me. And I really don't want to move to New York." Tim came over and Lorenzo thanked him for making sure they weren't bothered as Phillip exited. Lorenzo handed Tim a $50 bill and told him to give it to Anita for him.

"She'll be very happy to get this," Tim said. "I spoke to Dante and he said he'll start the paperwork for the license in the morning."

Lorenzo smiled. "Good. We'll talk when I get back from New York." He looked around at the busy restaurant. "Keep up the great work."

"I plan to," Tim responded.

Phillip was waiting for his car when Lorenzo got outside. It was obvious that he had something else on his mind as he handed the valet his claim ticket.

"For a man who's about to get a job offer from the number one label in the business, you look worried," Phillip said.

Lorenzo grimaced slightly. "Something Sylvia said is bugging me. 'You eat here often, don't you Lorenzo?' How do you figure she knew that? I mean, this isn't BOA or Katsuya where all the paparazzi and TMZ hang around waiting for people to come out."

"Well, if I had to guess, I'd say she had a background check done on you," Phillip said. "That's standard practice these days when you're hiring someone of your stature. Plus, you did pick the place." He looked at his phone before continuing. "Are you in town this weekend? We may need to do a deal memo before Monday."

Lorenzo held the door open for two women entering the restaurant. "Good evening ladies. Enjoy yourselves." Lorenzo turned his attention back to Philip. "I'm going to San Diego tomorrow for my high school reunion and I'll be there until Sunday. Just call or text me when you hear something," he said as he looked at his watch. "I've got to make a stop at Icy Gee's birthday party. You got any plans other than rushing home to your 'happy wife'?"

"Only to stay married for as long as possible," Phillip said.

Lorenzo smiled. "There's going to be strippers," he responded enticingly.

"Sounds tempting but, I'll pass. Sheila's waiting up for me. You have fun though."

"I always do Phil," Lorenzo said as he shook hands with Phillip and checked his phone for messages. "I always do." As Lorenzo and Phillip got into their cars and drove away, the man at the bar talked on his phone.

✹✹✹

As the Escalade sped southbound on the 405 freeway towards the airport, Sylvia talked on her phone. "He's definitely interested. Prepare

11

the offer sheet just as we discussed and send it to his attorney first thing in the morning. Make sure to include season tickets for his choice of the Knicks or Nets. By the way, the attorney says you have his cell number and can call him tonight if you want to." She listened. "No, I didn't mention that and I'm not going to unless I have to." She listened again before ending the call. "First thing in the morning, before you come into the office." Sylvia punched the end button on her phone and slid it into her bag. She slipped off her shoes, stretched out her shapely legs and put her pedicured feet on the console between the front and back seats. She leaned back in her seat and closed her eyes. The security man turned slightly in the front passenger seat and began to massage Sylvia's feet.

"Ahh," she purred as the lights of LAX came into view.

Chapter 3

Friday Morning

I t was a few minutes past 10 when Lorenzo swung his black 2012 BMW 650i convertible into the parking garage of the Beverly Hills building that housed the offices of Wilshire Records. He pulled into his reserved spot, turned off the engine and grabbed his phone and logo-free Louis Vuitton bag off the cream-colored passenger seat. Lorenzo had a taste for expensive luxury items, but he preferred the ones that didn't scream out, "Hey, I spent a lot of money for this."

As he rode the elevator to the 5th floor, Lorenzo ignored the rest of the passengers as he went over his schedule on his phone. It was a light morning since he was leaving for San Diego before lunch and that was good because he'd stayed at Icy Gee's party a bit longer than planned. When the elevator reached his floor, he stepped out into the lobby of Wilshire Records where he was immediately greeted by the label's head security man, Luther "Big" Barnes. Luther was a huge but not overweight former football player who in addition to taking care of security at Wilshire's offices, often body guarded their star artists when they were in town. As such, he'd been at last night's festivities, making sure things didn't get out of hand.

"Morning Mr. Taylor. I see you survived last night in one piece," Luther said with a huge smile on his face.

"Well 'Big', since I didn't get a phone call or text from you after I left and there weren't any breaking news stories this morning that included Icy's name, I'm going to assume that once again, you did your job."

Luther laughed. "That I did. Whatever happened in Strip City, stayed in Strip City."

"Which is where it belongs," Lorenzo laughed and exchanged a fist bump with Luther before heading to his office. He said hello to the receptionist as he breezed past her desk and headed down the hall. As he walked past one office, he heard a song that caught his ear. He stopped, stuck his head in the door and got the attention of the young staffer, "Money Mike" Morrison. "Yo Money, send me that so I can listen to it later on."

Morrison turned down the volume. "It's not the final mix. We're going back in this weekend to finish."

"Send it anyway. I want to hear it so in case I have any ideas, we can talk before you hit the studio," Lorenzo replied.

"Will do boss," Money said and cranked the volume back up.

Lorenzo continued down the hall and entered his corner office suite where his assistant Renee Brown was behind her desk in the outer office. Behind her, the door into Lorenzo's personal office was ajar and through the opening, Lorenzo could see there was someone sitting inside.

"Why is there someone in my office?" There was an edge to his voice.

Renee gave him a look and tone of voice that only a longtime, trusted assistant could get away with. "Good morning to you too." She nodded towards the door. "Arnold's waiting for you." She held up her left hand to cut him off. "Yes, I know you don't like people in your office when you're not here, but I've been keeping my eye on him. He hasn't touched anything."

Arnold Robertson's the head of business affairs for Wilshire and he and Lorenzo had clashed on several occasions over deals Lorenzo wanted to make.

Lorenzo sighed. "I'm really not in the mood for Arnold this morning. Any idea of what he wants?"

"He wouldn't say. The Michelle Casey contract is on your desk. You want coffee?"

"Yes please. And when you bring it, remind me that I have to get ready for a conference call in a few minutes."

Renee laughed. "I'm way ahead of you."

Lorenzo smiled and walked into his office which was decorated in earth tones and cream and furnished in a sleek, modern style. Outfitted with the latest in hi-tech audio-visual equipment, the platinum and gold CD plaques, awards and pictures of Lorenzo with recording artists, entertainers, athletes, politicians and other celebrities that lined the walls illustrated just how successful a career Lorenzo has had. Next to the couch, a cherry-red Gibson ES-335 guitar sat in a stand alongside a small amplifier and a Fender Rhodes electric piano. Photographs of a group of high school students at their graduation and one of a couple at a high school prom were prominently displayed on a credenza behind his desk. Lorenzo sat down behind his desk, pulled out a black and gold Mazurka pen and started signing the contract Renee had mentioned. As he wrote, he finally addressed Arnold Robertson. "What brings you out of your cave so early on a Friday morning Arnold? You need some fashion tips?"

Arnold, who even on 'Casual Friday' preferred the attire of the corporate lawyer he'd been before joining the label five years ago, ignored Lorenzo's sarcastic tone. "I need to talk to you about something very important and it can't wait."

"You could have talked to me last night if you had come to Icy's party. Which by the way, was off the chain! Even you could have got some play," Lorenzo sneered.

"You know I don't go to strip clubs. That kind of behavior isn't my style."

Lorenzo laughed and sat back in his swivel Aeron chair. "There were other bougie people there. There was a special section and everything. You would have felt right at home."

Renee entered with Lorenzo's coffee and handed it to him as he handed her the signed contract. "Don't forget you have that conference call at 10:30," she said.

"Thank you Renee."

"You're welcome. You want the door open or closed?"

"You can close it. I don't think Arnold's going to try and attack me." Lorenzo looked at Arnold. "Are you?"

"Renee, you didn't ask me if I wanted any coffee," a hurt sounding Arnold said.

Renee coolly turned to Arnold and said, "You're right; I didn't." She and Lorenzo exchanged sly smiles and she left the room as Arnold watched her close the door.

"Arnold, quit staring at Renee's ass and tell me why you're here," Lorenzo said coldly.

Arnold looked directly at Lorenzo. "I got a call at home last night from a friend. He said that he's hearing about some changes at Montclair Records."

Lorenzo's face was stoic but his mind was racing. "I didn't know you had any friends. Is there a new government program designed to help 'the friendless' that I haven't heard about?"

Arnold smiled sardonically. "I'll ignore your typically weak attempt at humor. Word on the street has it that they're looking for someone new to run their Urban Division and that Sylvia Andrews flew out here just to offer you the job."

"Is that right?" Lorenzo sipped his coffee as he tried to remain cool despite hearing that someone may have seen him and Phillip meeting with Sylvia last night.

"Well?"

"Well what?"

Frustrated and impatient, Arnold took the direct approach. "Are you talking to Sylvia Andrews about that job? Yes or no?"

"Arnold, why would I be talking to Sylvia Andrews or anybody about another job? I already have a job right here. One that I'm very happy with I might add." Lorenzo was determined to throw Arnold off his line of questioning.

"That's good to hear." Arnold changed the subject. "Debra and I are having some people over for brunch on Sunday. Why don't you drop by?"

"I'd love to," Lorenzo said as he lied through his teeth. Truth be told, he'd rather blow his brains out than spend an afternoon with Arnold and his equally snobbish wife. "But I can't do it. I've got other plans this weekend. I came in this morning just to sign Michelle Casey's contract. Which, by the way, needs your signature too before it goes to Josh."

"I'm well aware of what needs my signature around here," Arnold said smugly as he stared at Lorenzo. "I hope you're telling me the truth about Sylvia and Montclair Records."

"Arnold, why would I lie to you?"

"You have before."

Lorenzo smiled slightly. "True, but that was just to protect your dumb-ass from things you really didn't need to know."

Arnold stood and buttoned his suit coat.

"Don't forget to sign that contract and get it to Josh for his signature too," Lorenzo said as Arnold turned and left the office. He picked up his vibrating cell phone and read a new text message. It was from Lee Fleming, the editor of UrbanNationNews.com, the top-ranked black entertainment website. The message read, Is it true that you met with Sylvia Andrews last night? Jesus Christ, Lorenzo said to himself, this is getting out of hand. Lee wasn't in the habit of answering questions he didn't already know the answer to. He was just looking for confirmation. Lorenzo punched numbers into his phone as he walked over to the window that overlooked the street below. He had to find out who Arnold's source was and the sooner the better. He needed to nip this in the bud and fast.

Lorenzo spoke into the phone. "Is he in?" Lorenzo waited to be connected. "Yeah, this is Lorenzo. I need you to find out something for me." As he told the person on the other line what he needed, Lorenzo's mind was also on his trip to San Diego.

Chapter 4

Rancho Santa Fe, CA (north of San Diego)

The 10,000 square foot Tuscany-inspired villa that Patricia and Rudy Patterson along with their two children, Rudy Jr aka RJ and already 6'4 at 15 and 13 year-old Carmella, called home was hidden from the street by lush landscaping and a wall and electric gates at the end of a cul-de-sac. The estate's grounds included a multi-car garage, expansive lawns, lush gardens and fruit trees, a lagoon-style swimming pool, and lighted North-South tennis court with a regulation NBA basket at one end.

A very successful personal injury attorney turned venture capitalist and real estate developer, Rudolph "Rudy" Patterson had grown up in San Diego with Lorenzo. Rudy was one of the city's most successful African-American businessmen at the relatively young age of 38. Patricia Patterson nee Ruiz met Rudy when they were both students at San Diego State. Upon graduating from law school, Rudy went to work for a local firm while Patricia worked in public relations for the City of San Diego. After winning a record-setting personal injury lawsuit five years ago, he used his portion of the fee for a couple of high-risk investments that panned out and set Patricia and him up as multimillionaires.

Between the two of them, they now owned a law firm that specialized in personal-injury cases, a venture capital fund, a real estate development company and a very successful public relations and marketing firm, PRP Communications, which specialized in matching Hispanic-owned companies with consumers across the country.

Inside the sun drenched kitchen, RJ and Carmella cleared the breakfast dishes from the table as Patricia, wearing a brightly colored sundress and wedge slides, poured two cups of coffee. She put the coffee pot on the warmer and walked back to the table and sat down. Rudy sipped his coffee as he read the Wall Street Journal on his iPad.

The kids finished clearing the dishes and RJ said he was going outside to watch the workers put up the tent for the party and Carmella announced that she was going to Jennifer's house next door. As the kids left the room, Patricia leaned over and kissed Rudy on the mouth. He set his iPad down and reached for her with both hands. She laughed and playfully slapped them away.

"Stop it Rudy. Don't get me started this morning."

"'Stop it Rudy'? I was sitting here minding my own business when you leaned over and kissed me. How is that me starting anything?" Rudy had a mock pout on his face.

"All I did was give you a kiss," Patricia said.

"And all I did was try to touch my wife. Is there anything wrong with that?"

Patricia laughed. "No baby, there's nothing wrong with that. I just don't think it would be good for our children or housekeeper to walk in and find us having sex in the kitchen."

"It would be educational to say the least."

"Rudy!"

Rudy tried to act contritely. "What did I say?"

"What am I going to do with you?" Patricia got up from the table.

Rudy smacked her on the ass as she walked past him. "I catch you looking like this tonight, you'll going to have to do something with me.

"I'll keep that in mind."

Rudy smiled as he turned his attention back to his iPad and coffee. "You do that."

❈❈❈

Friday Afternoon

As he drove to San Diego, Lorenzo listened to the track that "Money Mike" sent him via the label's secure file-sharing server. He hated admitting it, but he couldn't find much that he'd change on it. He decided that should he actually end up leaving Wilshire, he'd tell Josh that Mike deserved a shot at running A&R.

Lorenzo used the car's hands-free feature to call and leave a message for Mike. "Money, this is Lorenzo. Just listened to the track. Not much I can say except that you nailed this one square on the head. My only suggestion is that you give the reverb on her vocal a half-turn back. Send me a text to let me know you got this message. I'll hear the final mix when I get back on Monday. Good job young man." Lorenzo paused before adding, "By the way, I signed her contract before I left the office today. Do me a favor and follow-up with Arnold to make sure he signs it today. Call me if he gives you any shade." Lorenzo ended the call and turned on the radio as he crossed the San Diego city line.

"This is Michelle Harris on XCEF 98.1. It's the weekend and for the King High School Class of 1993, it's reunion time. They're celebrating their 20 year reunion this weekend at the Marriott Marquis Hotel. As many of you know, I graduated from King in '95 so, I knew quite a few of the members of the Class of '93 including my brother Marvin. There are a few famous people in that class including noted talk show host Eddie Jackson who, according to my sources, will definitely be attending. Also in that class is County Supervisor Miguel Lopez, former baseball star Archie Watley and a legend in local legal circles, big-time lawyer and developer Rudy Patterson.

I also remember a guy named Ronnie Phillips from the class of '93. Who is Ronnie Phillips you ask? Well, he was simply the best athlete in the history of San Diego, that's all. He was All-County in football, basketball and track. And if he could have found time to play baseball, he'd have been All-County in that too.

But, like so many high school heroes, Ronnie ran into problems once he went to college and ended up leaving school without a degree or a chance to play in the pros. He dropped out of sight for a few years before drifting back to Diego, broke and strung out on drugs and alcohol. He ended up in trouble with the law and went away to prison for a while. He turned his life around in jail but by then it was too late. He'd contracted the AIDS virus somewhere along the way and two years ago, at the age of 36, Ronnie Phillips passed away.

Sending this one out to you Ronnie, wherever you are – 'It's So Hard To Say Goodbye To Yesterday' from Boyz II Men."

Lorenzo wiped tears from his eyes as he listened and drove on.

※❁※

Rudy, dressed in a lightweight V-neck sweater, slacks and loafers, walked into the kitchen to find Patricia talking to the caterer, celebrity chef Warren Graham, best known for his TV show *Cooking with Warren*. Through the windows overlooking the back yard, a group of workers erected a white tent as others unpacked dishes, glasses and silverware. "Hey Warren, try not to spend every dollar in the budget, okay?"

"I'll do my best Mr. Patterson, but the things your wife ordered don't come cheap."

Patricia turned to her husband. "Rudy, this is your reunion, your classmates. I'm just trying to make sure we show them how successful you are."

"I know. I was just joking. Sort of. Anyway, I'm going to run down to the hotel and check on things for tomorrow's dinner."

"Okay. Hey, do you mind stopping at the cleaners on your way back?"

"Isn't that Maria's job?" For reasons known only to him, Rudy absolutely detested even the thought of going to the cleaners. "You know I hate doing that."

Patricia walked up to her husband as Warren and two of his assistants continued making preparations. "I've got her so busy today, running all over town, she won't have time. Do this for me, okay? I'll make it up to you later on."

"I'm going to hold you to that promise."

"And you know I'll keep it," she purred seductively.

Rudy turned to walk away but was stopped by Patricia's hand on his arm. "Are you going to tell him?"

"No I'm not," he said shaking his head.

"Are you sure that's a good idea?"

"It doesn't matter if I think it's a good idea or not. I'm going to do what I was asked to do and that's it." Rudy paused and looked at his wife. "And you're not going to tell him either."

Patricia shook her head slightly. "No estoy de acuerdo con eso en absoluto. Él debe saber." (I don't agree with that at all. He should know.) Patricia had a habit of speaking Spanish when she wanted to stress her point with Rudy.

"Leave it alone Patricia," Rudy said forcefully.

"I will," she said a bit reluctantly.

Rudy kissed Patricia on her forehead and walked out and into the garage where the family's expensive automobiles sat. He walked past Patricia's silver Mercedes-Benz S55 sedan, the charcoal gray Range Rover and got into his baby blue Bentley Continental GTC.

Chapter 5

Phillip wore a wireless headset while he talked on the phone and practiced putting. "Lorenzo, this is Phillip."

It was an agitated Lorenzo who sat in his hotel suite overlooking San Diego Bay. "I've been trying to reach you all day. Arnold Robertson came to see me this morning before I left LA. Apparently, he's heard from some friend of his that I met with Sylvia last night. And, I got a text from Lee Fleming asking the same thing. How the hell did they find out so fast?"

Phillip laughed. "Hey, you're the one who picked the restaurant. But I wouldn't worry about Arnold or Lee because after you hear what I've got to say, all you'll need to worry about is whether to live in the city or New Jersey."

"I'm listening."

Phillip stopped putting, picked up a sheet of paper from his desk and read from it. "I talked with Weinberg this morning and here's what they're offering: three years at two million five per in annual salary with a 5% bump every year, stock options, three points on every act you sign, a generous expense account, money for your house payments in LA until you find a place in New York and here's the kicker: a $250,000 signing bonus."

"$250,000 just for signing the contract?"

"Just for signing your name on the dotted line."

Lorenzo didn't say anything.

Phillip chuckled to himself. "I believe this is the part where you say, 'Thank you Phillip for going out into one of the tightest job markets of the past few years and finding me a great new job with a significant pay raise at the number one label in the industry'. That's what you say now."

Lorenzo ignored what Philip said. "What about me staying out here?"

"Sylvia's willing to let you work out of LA one week a month but, you will have to move to New York. You heard what she said last night; she likes having her team around her."

"That's all well and good except that I'd rather live in LA."

"I know you hate New York, but it's pretty hard to live in Los Angeles when your job is back there," Phillip laughed as he resumed his putting.

"That's easy for you to say," Lorenzo shot back. "And for the record, I don't hate New York; I just prefer living in LA." He sighed. "Send me the offer sheet so I can look it over. Don't forget to send it to Ira too." Ira Goldman was Lorenzo's longtime business manager and the last word on all things financial in his life.

Phillip sank one last putt before he tossed his putter on the couch. "Will do. I'll be here all afternoon."

"One more thing Phil."

"What's that?"

"Thank you."

Phillip smiled. "Just doing what you pay me to do. And, you're welcome." He ended the call and walked back to his desk and punched the intercom button on the phone. "Beverly, come in here please."

Phillip's gorgeous assistant, the 5'10 and busty Beverly Johnson, dressed as always in an outfit that she could go straight from the office to Mr. Chow's and then a Hollywood club without changing, entered Phillip's office where he sat at his desk working on his Apple computer.

"I'm emailing the offer sheet from Montclair to Lorenzo Taylor and Ira Goldman. I blind copied you. Make sure you read it and know all the details."

Beverly walked behind Philip and massaged his neck and shoulders. "I always do."

Phillip sent the email and leaned back in his chair. "What's on my schedule for this afternoon?"

"You have a conference call at 4 with Aaron Brown's accountant and manager to discuss his upcoming royalty audit. And Graham Armstead called about his pre-nup."

Phillip leaned his head back to get a better view of Beverly's tantalizing cleavage. "Make sure Rich Macnow from the tax department is here for the call and check on the pre-nup with Nancy in family law."

"Okay. By the way, your wife called while you were on with Lorenzo. She wants to know if you got those Rhianna tickets for her niece. She's on her cell."

"Ahhh," Phillip enjoyed Beverly's touch. "Call Lon over at Staples Center and ask him to set that up for me."

Beverly reached over Phillip's shoulders, unbuttoned his shirt and ran her French-tipped manicured fingers down his chest.

"I hope you remembered to lock the door," Phillip said.

Beverly laughed that sexy, throaty laugh that Phillip loved so much. "Of course I did," she purred as her tongue worked its way from his left ear and down his neck.

Chapter 6

Lorenzo sat at the suite's dining table using his iPad to read the email from Phillip. His attorney had indeed told him the truth; it was a great offer. Except for the part where he'd have to move to New York City, it was almost perfect, especially his being able to spend more time in the studio. He knew what Sylvia had said about preferring to have her team around her, but maybe there was some flexibility in that area that Phillip could explore. His reading was interrupted by a knock on the door to the suite.

Lorenzo called out "Who is it?" with his eyes glued to the tablet's screen.

"Room service, sir."

"Room service?" Lorenzo was puzzled. "I didn't order anything from room service."

Lorenzo stood up and walked over to the door. When he looked through the peephole and saw Rudy standing there, he opened the door with a huge smile on his face.

Rudy laughed. "Close your mouth son! You look like you just saw Beyonce or Halle Berry naked out in the hall."

Rudy and Lorenzo hugged as they both burst out in laughter.

"I've seen one of them naked and that's all I'm gonna say. What are you doing here?"

"Are you going to let me in or do I have to stand in the hallway?"

Lorenzo stepped aside to let his best friend in life enter the suite and closed the door behind them. They walked into the living room and sat down, Rudy on the couch and Lorenzo in the easy chair.

"Well, as you know, I'm the dinner chairman and I needed to check on a few things with the banquet manager. Plus, the caterer's at the house and he and Patricia are figuring out more ways to spend money so," Rudy shrugged, "I decided to take a ride."

Lorenzo laughed again. "Things are that bad huh?"

"Man, you know I love my wife dearly. But, I don't want to be around her when she's getting things ready for a party."

"Must be her Latina blood coming out."

Rudy smiled. "Her Latina blood comes out in other and much better ways, thank you very much. No, this is her latent drill sergeant gene rearing its ugly head as it does in situations like this."

"Speaking of Patricia, how's her company doing these days?" Lorenzo asked.

"It's doing fine. They've expanded into several other markets. Ramon opened the Austin office last year." Ramon is Patricia's son from a previous relationship who'd stayed there after earning his MBA from the University of Texas.

"That's good to hear." Lorenzo shook his head. "Man, can you believe it's been twenty years since we graduated from King? It seems like it was only yesterday that we were marching across that stage on the football field. Where did the time go?"

"Some days it doesn't seem like it's been that long and then other days, it seems even longer. But, here we are twenty years later. All growed up and everything." Rudy looked around the room. "Where are your golf clubs? Or did you forget that we're playing in the morning?"

"They're in my car. You want something to drink?" Lorenzo stood and walked over to the mini-bar.

Rudy leaned back on the couch. "A Diet Coke if you've got it. Easy on the ice."

Lorenzo poured soda into two glasses, added a few cubes of ice to each and walked back to where Rudy sat. He handed Rudy one glass and then sat back down with the other.

"I was listening to the radio on the way in. The DJ was talking about Ronnie."

"Who was the DJ?"

"Michelle Harris. Said she was a couple years behind us at King."

Rudy mused. "That must be Marvin Harris' sister. I think she had a thing for Ronnie back in the day."

"Wait a minute. That green-eyed girl with the deep voice and big ass?"

"That's the one."

"Oh yeah, I remember her chasing after him. Anyway, she mentioned you too. Called you a 'legend in local legal circles'."

Rudy seemed a bit amused at being called a legend. "That's funny considering I'm rarely actually in court these days." He sipped from his glass. "What did she say about Ronnie?"

"She talked about what a great athlete he was. And how he flunked out of college, got hooked on drugs and alcohol and died from AIDS two years ago."

"Well Chocks, that's pretty much what happened to him. Chapter and verse."

Lorenzo sipped his drink and shook his head. "He should have never left San Diego for college. Ronnie just wasn't ready to be out there on his own. All he ever wanted to do was play sports, chase girls and be liked by everybody."

"True."

"I've always wondered what would have happened if he'd been around us. We could have made sure he stayed on the right path."

Rudy shrugged his shoulders. "Maybe, maybe not. Look, I loved Ronnie as much as you did but, he made his choices just like the rest of us. Unfortunately, by the time he decided to change his life, he had AIDS and it was too late."

"You're probably right."

"Damn right I am." Rudy leaned forward. "You can't save somebody from themselves if they don't want to be saved. Believe me, I learned that lesson a long time ago with my brother."

"You're right." Lorenzo sighed. "But, Ronnie was something else."

Rudy leaned back on the couch. "Best athlete I've ever seen."

"Me too."

Both men were quiet for a minute.

Rudy decided to change the subject. "So, what's new with you these days?"

"Well, I've been offered a job at Montclair Records in New York and I'm thinking about taking it."

Rudy didn't hide the surprise on his face or in his voice. "I thought you hated New York."

Lorenzo shook his head. "I don't know where people got the idea that I hate New York. I'd just rather live in LA where the winters, for the most part, are nice and warm."

"I know this isn't my area of expertise" Rudy said, "but don't most record companies have offices in Los Angeles?"

"Some still do and Montclair has one that my lawyer says I can work from one week out of the month. But, I'd have to spend most of my time in New York. Things have really changed in the last few years and most of the power is back there now. Plus, the woman who's trying to hire me, Sylvia Andrews, likes having her team near her." Lorenzo sighed. "So, unless you've got your own label like a Jay-Z or somebody like that, you follow the check."

"Well, have you ever thought about starting your own label?"

"Yeah, I've thought about it, but it takes a lot of money to get started and then you need to get a distribution deal, sign artists and record their albums. Then, there's promotion, tour support, etc, etc." Lorenzo shook his head. "There's a lot more to the music business besides music. Besides, the contract from Montclair ain't too shabby. I get to spend more time producing artists and hell, they're including a $250,000 signing bonus. How can I turn down that kind of money?"

Rudy shrugged his shoulders. "That's not a lot of money when you really think about it."

"Maybe not to you, but a quarter of a million dollars is still quite a bit to me. Of course, you're the one with the estate, Bentley and God only knows what else considering what Patricia brings in. So maybe that's chump change to you, but it's not to me."

"I thought you got a nice 'taste' when your company was sold last year."

"I did, but after I paid off my house, my business manager put the rest away in my retirement fund," Lorenzo said. "As far as I'm concerned, that money doesn't even exist."

Rudy pushed forward. "Look, this isn't my world but Carmella's a big fan of Taylor Swift and we went to her concert last summer. A few weeks later, there's a big story on her in Forbes magazine about how she got started with a tiny little label in Nashville when she was only 16. The guy that owns her label was just like you; he'd been at a big company and left it to start his own. She was one of the first people he signed and now she's one of the biggest entertainers in the world."

"You think you're telling me something I don't know?" Lorenzo laughed. "Man, I know the Taylor Swift story backward and forward," he said. "Did the article mention that her father's a big-time stockbroker who invested in the company too? Let me tell you this Rudy, just in case you don't know it, damn near everybody in my position dreams about finding a 'Taylor Swift' of their own. Only one problem: there's not too many out there with her songwriting and singing talents."

"Maybe not, but my point is, if that guy in Nashville could do it, why can't you? Hell, I can get you the money if that's your hang-up." Rudy glanced at Lorenzo's open briefcase and spotted a medicine bottle and a 9 millimeter handgun before he spoke again. "You make plenty of money now; you've got power, respect. You've got a nice house, a couple of cars, a condo in Cabo and vacation all over the world. Hell, a few years ago you were even a bachelor of the year in Ebony."

"Yeah and I got some good pussy behind that too," Lorenzo laughed.

"But, I look in your briefcase and I see medication for an ulcer. And you haven't had a serious relationship since, what was that stripper's name?"

"Uvanda."

Rudy nodded. "Right and that was two years ago. This might not be any of my business but I gotta ask you; are you happy with the way things are? Would a new job and moving to New York really change anything?"

Lorenzo stood up and walked over to the window and stared out at the San Diego harbor. He stood there silently for a minute before he responded. "That's a damn good question. By the way, strippers need love too."

"I'll take your word on that." Rudy paused. "Do you know what she's doing these days?"

Lorenzo smiled. "Believe it or not, she's in college studying to become an accountant."

"I guess anything's possible," Rudy said. "But you didn't answer my other question."

Lorenzo turned and looked at his best friend. "I honestly don't know."

"Why do you have a gun?" Rudy asked.

Lorenzo sat back down. "Hey man, LA is still the carjacking capitol of the free world and I drive a nice car. Plus, it doesn't hurt to be careful in the music business, if you know what I mean." He could tell Rudy was concerned. "Don't worry Mr. Lawyer, it's registered and I have a concealed weapons permit."

"So, what's your next move?" Rudy asked.

"I guess I'm going to sign the contract with Montclair and get ready to move my ass to New York. Who knows, maybe moving will be good for me. There's a lot going on there these days. Besides, what else can I do? Music is all I really know."

"That's true," Rudy agreed. "But, and don't laugh, you could always come and work with me."

"Yeah, right. Frankly, I'm not sure what it is that you really do besides make money."

Rudy looked directly at Lorenzo. "I'm serious; I could teach you the development game. It's not exactly rocket science."

"Thanks but, I'm a music man. That's what I know and do best."

※⊗※

After Rudy left the suite, Lorenzo called Phillip and gave him his instructions. He was to call Jeffrey Weinberg and let him know that he needed a few days to decide and he'd like to meet with Sylvia when he was in New York on Thursday. Also, Phillip was to have a letter delivered to Arnold Robertson that afternoon officially notifying Wilshire of Montclair's offer and giving them three business days to match. Phillip was skeptical that Josh's bosses in Tokyo would allow him to do so, especially on such short notice, but Lorenzo was the client and what the client wanted was what Phillip always did his best to make happen. In the meantime, Lorenzo would reach out to Lee Fleming and see if he could convince him to sit on the story for the time being.

The clock was officially ticking.

Chapter 7

Preparations were in full swing at Rudy and Patricia's for the reunion kickoff party. The tennis court had been tented, tables and chairs set out and workers went about their assigned chores as Patricia made sure everyone did their jobs. "I want the food ready and on the buffet line at 7 sharp. You understand me Warren?"

"Yes Mrs. Patterson. That won't be a problem. The food will be ready for serving at 7."

"I'll hold you personally responsible if it's not."

RJ walked up to his mother. "They won't let me in the kitchen and I'm hungry. Can I have something to eat?"

"How can you be hungry? I saw you eat two big plates of spaghetti at lunch."

"Moms, that was almost three hours ago," an exasperated RJ said.

Warren overheard and walked over. "I can fix him a plate in the kitchen Mrs. Patterson."

"Yeah Warren, hook a brotha up!"

Patricia glanced at her son before she turned to the caterer. "I don't want you distracted Warren. He's not the one who's paying you."

"It's not a problem at all. Everything is under control," Warren said as he waved his right arm around to get Patricia to take in all that was going on.

Patricia looked around and seemingly satisfied by what she saw, she relaxed just a bit. "Okay Warren. Sorry if I'm stressing you, but I just want everything to be perfect tonight."

"No problem. I understand. And don't worry, things are going to be spectacular."

"I know they will. RJ, where's your sister?"

RJ walked towards the house with Warren. "Where she always is, in her room texting."

※※

Beverly Hills

Josh Evans, the founder and chairman of Wilshire Records, sat in his memento-laden office and listened as Arnold Robertson ran through their options after reviewing Phillip's letter. While it was true that Lorenzo had been working without a contract while Wilshire's Japanese owners reviewed the label's operations from top to bottom, Josh never thought for a minute that his protégé, the guy he'd discovered during a studio session 10 years ago and mentored ever since, would consider leaving the only professional home he'd ever had. Especially not to work for Sylvia Andrews whom Josh believed symbolized the soulless new corporate structure in the music business to the nth degree. At his core, Josh remained a man in love with music and had disdain for executives like Sylvia, who'd come to the music business from the corporate world.

"I say let Lorenzo go. There's no way we should ask Tokyo for permission to match an offer like this," Arnold concluded and sat back in his chair. "This is an opportunity to reshape things more along the lines of what Wanatabe is sure to want when their review is finished. 'Money Mike' can handle A&R just fine."

"Arnold, I appreciate your in-depth analysis. I know you've given it a lot of careful thought," Josh smiled sardonically. "I also know that you and Lorenzo have had your differences in the past and you'd love to see him gone from here. But here's the thing you don't fully grasp: I can replace you in fifteen minutes without missing a beat. There are literally dozens of lawyers in this town who can do what you do. But creative guys like Lorenzo, ah, they don't grow on trees. Don't get me wrong; 'Money Mike' is a talented guy who might grow into a very valuable asset to this company someday. But right now," Josh shook his shaggy head, "he's not ready to replace Lorenzo no matter what you may think."

Arnold was taken aback by Josh's brutally frank assessment of his position on the Wilshire Records food chain, so he was extra-careful with his response. "Yes Josh, I do have a problem with Lorenzo always wanting to give away the farm to artists, particularly brand-new ones without a track record. But this isn't about that. This is about doing what's best for the label long-term."

Arnold took another sheet of paper out of a file folder and handed it to Josh. "I had my own financial guy run the numbers. Even allowing for the low-end on sales with Lorenzo as a producer on three projects a fiscal year, this is what we'd be paying him."

Josh whistled. "That's more than I make."

"Exactly."

"Of course, I am sitting on the $850 million that I got when I sold the company to Wanatabe," Josh chuckled. "So I've got that to fall back on."

"We all benefitted from the sale and you took care of Lorenzo quite nicely if I recall correctly." Arnold was still bitter that he'd received less than half of what Josh gave Lorenzo when the sale went through.

"Maybe I should have done more." Josh sighed as he looked over the document again. "If Lorenzo made that kind of money under that same deal here, that means the label would be doing very well, right?"

Arnold nodded. "True. It would probably also mean his sitting in your seat one day and you wondering how it happened."

"Hmm, I never looked at it that way. But guess what; I'm not worried about that happening. I may not own this label anymore, but I founded it in my garage 40 years ago and I think I still have a better idea of what's good for it than anyone else. So here's what I want you to do: nothing. Don't call his lawyer or Lorenzo until you hear from me.

I'm going to call him myself and see if we can work things out." The forceful tone in Josh's voice was unmistakable.

"With all due respect Josh, I don't think that's a good idea," Arnold said. "After all, Lorenzo didn't call you before having Phillip Walker send over that letter."

Josh smiled. "With all due respect Arnold, I don't give a damn what you think is a good idea right now. This is between me and Lorenzo."

Arnold pushed back one more time. "What about Tokyo? Somebody needs to let Yoshi know what's going on." Yoshi Nakamura was the label's liaison with Wanatabe Industries, Wilshire's parent company.

"Let me worry about Yoshi," Josh said. "I'll let you know when I need you to worry about something," he added in a very dismissive tone.

Chapter 8

Friday Evening

Lorenzo pulled his car up to the parking valet station at the end of Patricia and Rudy's driveway and gave his name to a security guard holding a clipboard. The other guests would have their vehicles parked for them and be driven up to the house in golf carts, but the guard told him to park by the garage. Lorenzo gave the guard a $20 bill and smiled as he drove onto the property. It was just one of the perks of lifelong friendship. He parked his car, raised the top and climbed out, dressed from head to toe in all-white as the invitation specified. His phone vibrated and when he looked at the screen, he saw the message wasn't the news he'd been waiting on – No word yet on Arnold's spy. Will keep digging if you want me to. BTW, found out that Sylvia Andrews tried to hire you in 2010 but Josh Evans refused to give her permission to talk to you.

Lorenzo, visibly surprised by the last sentence, texted back: Are you sure about 2010?

The response was almost immediate. 100%. I've got a copy of the letter. What about the other thing?

Lorenzo texted back. No need. It doesn't matter now. Send your invoice and a copy of that letter to the usual place. Thanks.

Whoever Arnold and Kevin used to find out about Lorenzo and Phillip's meeting with Sylvia was a ghost and like Phillip had said earlier that afternoon, it didn't really matter anymore. But the news that

Sylvia had tried to hire him three years ago was a shock to him. He'd have to talk to Phillip and see what he knew about that.

As Lorenzo walked up the front steps, the door opened and RJ came out to greet him.

"What's up Uncle Lorenzo?"

"Hey RJ. How's my favorite basketball player doing these days?" They exchanged a 'man-hug' and fist bump.

"I'm good and so is my game."

"Glad to hear that. Where's everybody else?"

"Pops is getting dressed, Carmella's in her room and Moms is getting stuff ready for tonight. Word of advice; stay out of her way until the party starts. She's on fire right now."

Lorenzo laughed. "That's exactly what your father said earlier today."

"He wasn't lying."

Lorenzo and RJ walked into the entry hall of the house. Carmella ran down the staircase and jumped into Lorenzo's arms and kissed him on the cheek.

"Hey Uncle Lorenzo!"

"Hey little girl. How's my favorite goddaughter?"

Carmella dropped to the floor and put her hands on her hips. "I'd better be your only goddaughter."

"You are the only one," Lorenzo laughed. "Lord knows I couldn't handle another one like you."

RJ rolled his eyes and muttered. "Neither could anyone else."

Carmella shot her brother a withering look. "Zip it basketball boy."

Lorenzo laughed. "Where's your mother?"

"In the kitchen, but I wouldn't go in there if I were you," Carmella warned.

RJ agreed. "She's right for once; stay out here where it's safe."

"I think I can handle your mother after knowing her for all these years," Lorenzo said as he walked down the hall.

RJ and Carmella exchanged a glance as Lorenzo headed for the kitchen.

"Don't say we didn't warn you!" Carmella yelled. She turned to her brother, "He's dead meat."

"We warned him. Whatever happens is on him," RJ said.

✖✖

After his meeting with Josh, it was a shaken and chastened Arnold Robertson who retreated to his office to plan his next move. Tipping off Lee Fleming had turned out to be a dead end once it became clear that Lorenzo wasn't going to take the bait. He knew it had been a longshot considering Josh and Lorenzo's long history together, but he'd hoped to convince Josh to let him handle the negotiations with Lorenzo and Phillip on his own. However, that wasn't to be the case as Josh had just made it abundantly clear that this was now between him and Lorenzo. Arnold had one more trick up his sleeve, but it was a risky one, one that if not handled properly, could put his own job at risk. Maybe his wife had been right last night when she suggested that he take a step back, let things develop on their own, and he'd have Lorenzo out of his hair once and for all.

✖✖

The kitchen was full of people and activity when Lorenzo reached it and looked around. Lorenzo stood near the doorway and called out to get Patricia's attention. "Hey Ruiz!" he yelled, using his old pet name for her.

Patricia looked up at the sound of her maiden name. "Hey Lorenzo. Come give me a kiss."

Lorenzo picked his way through the swarm of workers and made his way over to Patricia and Warren. They hugged and kissed each other on the cheek before Patricia turned to Warren.

"Warren, this is our good friend Lorenzo Taylor. He and Rudy grew up together."

Lorenzo shook's Warren outstretched hand. "We've met before. I used to eat at your restaurant all the time."

43

"Yes you did," Warren said. "In fact, as I recall, you were one of my best customers. If I'd had a few more like you, I could have kept the place open."

"Maybe now that the economy's better, you can open another spot," Lorenzo said.

Warren smiled. "That's what I'm working on. In fact, I've been lining up investors. In the meantime, I'm doing private parties like this and the show on Food Planet to keep my name out there. Maybe you'd be interested in seeing the business plan."

"Sure, I'm always looking for a good investment," Lorenzo said as he handed Warren his business card. "Give me a call and we'll get together."

"I'll definitely do that." Warren was beaming.

"I'm hoping to convince Rudy to invest in Warren's next venture. That's one of the reasons I hired him for tonight," Patricia said before she shifted gears. "But right now Warren, please make sure the shrimp are iced down properly."

"It's already taken care of. And I've got the extra crab legs you wanted."

Lorenzo laughed. "Damn Sgt. Patterson, lighten up for a minute and relax. This man knows what he's doing."

Lorenzo took Patricia by the arm and led her over to the table on the other side of the kitchen where they sat down.

"So tell me, how are you doing?"

"I'm fine," Patricia said as she tossed her head back and her luxurious mane of black hair swayed from side to side.

"I know you're fine. What I want to know is how you're doing."

Patricia smiled and squeezed Lorenzo's left hand for a brief moment. "Lorenzo, I'm doing great and life couldn't be better. Thanks for asking." Patricia turned to see what was going on across the room but before she could say anything, Rudy entered the room.

"Remind me again whose bright idea it was for everyone to wear all-white tonight."

Patricia ran her eyes up and down her husband's lean body and said, "It was my idea and it was a good one. Isn't that right Lorenzo?"

"Well…"

"Don't encourage him," Patricia said. "Both of you know it's a great idea."

Rudy sat down at the table with them. "You two aren't sitting in my kitchen trying to figure out how to get rid of me so you can run off together are you?"

"Rudy, as much as I love Lorenzo, you know that you're all the man I'll ever need or want."

"Besides," Lorenzo laughed, "I can't afford her."

Rudy laughed right along with Lorenzo and Patricia. "Hell, I barely can. And that's even with her money added in."

"You knew I was high-maintenance when you met me," Patricia said.

Rudy leaned over and kissed his wife's lips. "That's true. And frankly, I wouldn't want you any other way. So, has anybody else besides this bigheaded boy arrived?"

"No, he's the only one so far. Oh, I forgot to tell you; Reese called and said he'll be here around 8."

Rudy stood up. "Good. Come on Chocks, let's go outside. God knows it's got to be quieter out there."

Patricia immediately turned her attention back to the preparations on the other side of the room. "Warren…"

Chapter 9

Lorenzo and Rudy stepped out onto the patio. They each got a drink from the bartender, walked out by the pool which had a huge "Class of 1993" ice sculpture floating in it and sat down on the chaise lounges flanking the west side of the pool. The outdoor lights had taken effect and the house and grounds shimmered as security guards patrolled discreetly.

Lorenzo looked around and sipped his drink. "The security guards are a nice touch but, are they really necessary?"

"I know most of the people we went to school with but, you can't tell about some of their husbands and wives. I don't plan on anything stupid jumping off at my house."

"I feel ya," Lorenzo said.

"How's your pops doing these days? He enjoying his retirement?"

Lorenzo nodded his head. "He's good. I was in Vegas last month and spent a couple of days with him. He seems happier than he has been in a long time. He and Louise bought a nice house on a golf course. How are your folks doing in Memphis?"

"They seem to be okay. I think my mother's bored out of her mind, but since it was her idea to move, she'll never admit it." Rudy looked at Lorenzo and knew there was something on his mind.

"Rudy, can I ask you a personal question?"

"You can ask me anything. You know that," Rudy said as he sipped his drink.

Lorenzo placed his glass on the table between the chaise lounges before he spoke. "You wanted to be a lawyer since we were kids right?"

"Since I was sixteen years old."

"And you met Patricia when you were nineteen, right?"

"You were standing right there the first time I saw her," Rudy said. "Where are you going with this?"

Lorenzo turned to look directly at his best friend. "Have you ever wondered what your life would be like if you hadn't met Patricia when you did?"

Before Rudy could answer, a guard walked up to them. "Excuse me Mr. Patterson. Mrs. Patterson said to tell you that your guests are starting to arrive."

"Thank you Jamal. Tell her I'll be right there."

"Yes sir." Jamal talked into his security mouthpiece as he walked away.

Rudy stood up and straightened his clothes. "I have to go and play gracious host now, but we can finish this later if you want."

"Yeah."

Patricia's voice came across the yard. "Rudy, I need you."

"It must be nice to have someone need you." Lorenzo said.

Rudy smiled as he turned and walked away. "It is."

Lorenzo leaned back into the chaise lounge and sipped his drink. Maybe moving to New York could be a new start personally as well as professionally he thought to himself.

❊❊

Outside, a black Cadillac sedan pulled up to the valet parking station and the driver's door was opened by the waiting attendant. A woman dressed in an above-the-knee length white cocktail dress and strappy Jimmy Choo sandals with four-inch heels took her claim ticket from the valet and walked to the waiting golf cart. The valet, momentarily stunned into silence by her breathtaking beauty, found his voice and greeted her. Smiling, she returned his greeting and slid onto the padded leather seat next to him. Slyly admiring her long legs and luscious figure, the driver pressed the accelerator and the cart moved forward.

※※

The tent was crowded with people as the party was in full swing. Charles Reid and his wife Chris were there, dressed to the nines as usual. Alvin Brooks, fat and bald, was there as well as were the aforementioned Marvin Harris and Eddie Jackson who had a crowd three-deep around him. Lorenzo was talking to DeWitt Stewart and his wife Jacqueline when Rudy came up and whispered in his ear, "There's someone waiting in the living room to see you."

"Who?"

Rudy smiled. "Go into the living room and see for yourself."

Lorenzo excused himself, turned and headed into the house and as he walked into the living room, he saw a woman looking at the family pictures displayed on the mantel above the fireplace. She turned when she heard Lorenzo walk into the room, their eyes met and they stared at each other. It was the same woman who'd arrived in the black Cadillac.

Chapter 10

"Hello Lorenzo."

Lorenzo was frozen in place. Tina Davis was the absolute last person he expected to see when he walked into the room.

"Tina? What are you doing here? Rudy didn't tell me that you were coming this weekend."

"I told him not to say anything. I wanted to surprise you."

Lorenzo shook his head. "This is the best surprise I've had in a long time." He looked her up and down. "Damn, you look good!"

"Why thank you Lorenzo," Tina laughed. "You don't look too bad yourself."

They hugged and kissed each other on the cheek before they sat down next to each other on a sofa. Unbeknownst to them, Rudy peeked into the room from the doorway, saw them sitting together, turned and walked away with a big smile on his face. He'd done his part; the rest was up to them.

"So, Rudy tells me that you've become quite a big shot in the music business over the last few years."

Lorenzo smiled before he responded. "Well, I'm a vice president at Wilshire Records."

"Don't be so modest. I've Googled you and everything I've read says you're one of the top people in your field. Rudy even says you should be a judge on one of those singing shows."

"Sometimes Rudy talks too much." Lorenzo paused. "Or in this case, not enough."

"He's very proud of you," Tina said. "You're like a brother to him."

Lorenzo nodded. "He's the best friend I've ever had. But, that's enough about me. Why didn't you want me to know you were going to be here tonight?"

Before Tina could answer, Lorenzo's cell phone vibrated. He looked at it, saw the name Josh Evans, then excused himself and walked out into the entryway.

✖☉✖

Lorenzo and Josh talked to each other via the FaceTime feature on their iPhones. "I hope I'm not bothering you Lorenzo. Renee told me that you're in San Diego for a reunion this weekend."

"No bother at all Josh. Frankly, I was hoping to hear from you tonight."

"Well, I guess you know why I'm calling."

"I told Phillip that I wanted to give you a chance to match Sylvia's offer. After all you've done for my career, I figured I owed you that much even though I've been working without a contract and could just walk away, free and clear."

Josh sighed. "You know how things are with Tokyo right now. I've pushed them as hard as I can to finish their review, but they work at their own pace. Frankly, if I didn't have two more years left on my contract…Anyway, I know Sylvia's made you a great offer, but are you sure Montclair is the kind of company you want to work for? They don't care about building careers for their artists. All they worry about is the next hot thing and the bottom line. We're still all about the music at Wilshire."

Now it was time for Lorenzo to put his cards on the table. "I can appreciate all of that Josh but, fact is, our market share has declined the past few years. Look, I'd love to stay. You know how I feel about the company; you, the people, our artists, the traditions, everything. Hell, I might not even have a career if it weren't for you. But, I have to look

52

at what's best for me now both personally and professionally. Plus, the business is changing with all the new technology coming in and after this review, who knows what the future will look like at Wilshire. I don't want to be on the outside looking in because your new bosses won't invest more resources in the label."

"I can't argue with anything you've said Lorenzo and frankly, it's pretty much what I figured you would say after you talked with Sylvia," Josh responded. "Believe me, I'd love to match the offer but I just can't. At least not dollar for dollar. Besides, you already have a nice lifestyle. How much money does a single man like you really need?"

Lorenzo was slightly angered by Josh's last question and there was an edge to his voice when he responded.

"That's easy for you to say Josh. I'm not the one who got almost a billion dollars for selling the company, living in Malibu and riding to work in a chauffeur-driven Rolls Royce when you do come into the office these days."

Josh smiled. "Touche. Well, I just hope that you'll give me one last chance before you make your final decision. The production clause is a little rich for our blood and I doubt that I can sell it to Tokyo. Maybe there are some other things that we can do to keep you in the Wilshire family. Your own label or something like that."

"I'll keep that in mind. Maybe if you put that in writing and sent it over to Phillip…"

"I'll talk to your good friend Arnold and tell him to convey that to Phillip. I'll be in the office on Monday. Let's talk again then."

Lorenzo laughed. "I'm not sure if that's how I'd describe him, but Arnold and Phillip seem to be able to speak to each other on decent enough terms."

"It's not all Arnold's fault. I pay him to be the bad cop. You know that."

"Maybe so, but I've got to be honest with you Josh; lately, he really seems to enjoy it."

Now it was Josh who laughed. "He is well suited for the role, I'll give you that. Have fun at your reunion and I'll see you Monday."

"I will Josh and thanks for calling personally. It means a lot."

"However this turns out Lorenzo, I will always treasure our friendship."

"So will I Josh, so will I."

They ended the call and as Josh's image faded from his phone, Lorenzo sighed and exhaled deeply. Well, he thought to himself as he walked through the house headed for the party outside, both sides know where they stood now. He passed a couple of partygoers and overheard one of them say, "What kind of lawyer can afford a place like this **and** Warren Graham as a caterer?" Lorenzo stopped, took a couple of prawns off one of their plates, smiled and said, "A very rich one" before he continued on his way.

Chapter 11

The DJ was spinning songs from their school years when Lorenzo entered the tent and looked for Tina. He finally spotted her talking to Dana Jamerson and began walking in that direction. But before he could reach her, the hefty Helen Lacey grabbed his arm and pulled him out onto the dance floor.

After three songs, Lorenzo finally pulled himself away from Helen, grabbed a glass of ice water from the bar and walked over to where Rudy was talking to their friend Reese Ellis. Lorenzo and Reese greeted each other warmly.

"Damn," Reese laughed. "I thought Helen wasn't going to ever let you go!"

"Me either. Whew! That girl has enough ass for two women!" Lorenzo said as he laughed and drank his water. He then turned to Rudy and asked him, "Why didn't you tell me?"

Rudy shrugged and sipped his drink. "She wanted to surprise you."

"Well, she sure did that."

Reese looked around the tent. "Where's DeWitt? I just saw him a minute ago."

"He's over there talking to Hector Torres," Lorenzo said as he pointed across the tent before he turned back to Rudy. "You still could have told me."

"I could have, but where would the fun in that have been?"

Reese leaned back in between the two of them. "I hate to break up whatever it is that you two are rambling on about, but is that woman with her arm around Hector young enough to be his daughter?"

"She's young but not that young," Rudy said as he waved to get DeWitt's attention. "Besides, didn't you marry a 25 year old swim suit model last year?"

Lorenzo looked at Reese. "Speaking of which, where is your new wife?"

"Well, if you must know, Vanessa's on a photo shoot in Puerto Rico. But I tell you what, I bet you both a hundred bucks that girl with Hector is under 25."

Rudy wasted no time in saying "I'll take that bet" as did Lorenzo. As they exchanged fist bumps to seal the bets, DeWitt walked up with a look of amusement on his face. "You're not going to believe this, but that's Hector's third wife and get this: she's only 24 years old!"

Without a word, Lorenzo and Rudy both reached into a pant pocket, pulled out some cash and handed Reese a hundred dollar bill.

"Thank you gentlemen. Nice doing business with you both."

A puzzled DeWitt looked at the three men. "Did I miss something?"

"No, not really," Lorenzo said.

"Well, Reverend Stewart, now that you've blessed us with your presence, let's get a picture of the old gang," Rudy said as he motioned for the photographer to come over.

"Careful Rudy," Reese said. "He knows God personally."

"Thank you brother Ellis, I'll keep that in mind," Rudy said.

✖⊕✖

After more dancing and catching up with old friends, Lorenzo and Tina finally got a chance to talk and they both promised not to leave the party without speaking again. At Rudy's insistence the fellas moved their private gathering into the game room. The four lifelong friends ate and drank while getting caught up with each other as highlights from ESPN played silently on the 70" Vizio flat screen TV mounted on the wall. Lorenzo told them that he's thinking about changing jobs and moving to New York, Rudy talked about a project he's developing and how he told his staff to leave him alone this weekend unless it's an emergency that only he can handle, Reese announced that he's about to become a regional Vice-President at Coca-Cola and DeWitt said that he's working on a book of inspirational essays for men. DeWitt teased Reese about not bringing his new wife to the reunion and Reese responded by asking, "Who sweats more while preaching: you or T.D. Jakes?"

"Probably him," Dewitt said as they all laughed. "He's a lot bigger than me."

As the evening wound down, Rudy changed the subject. "Can you guys be on time in the morning? I'm paying the green fees and you're not going to waste my money by being late. Be on time just this once and I'll be very happy."

"I know you're not talking to me," Lorenzo said. "I'm always on time. You must be talking to the 'late twins' over there" as he gestured towards DeWitt and Reese.

DeWitt laughed sarcastically. "Ha, ha. The 'late twins', that's a good one Chocks. But seriously, what are a few green fees to a rich man like Rudy?"

"That's how rich people stay rich D," Reese interjected. "They watch every damn penny, let alone the dollars. Plus, I bet he got an early-bird discount."

"Just be on time. That's all I'm asking you guys to do."

❊❂❊

Lorenzo stood next to Tina as she waited for a golf cart to take her down the driveway.

"Where are you staying?" Lorenzo asked.

"I'm living at my parents' house for now, but I'm staying at the Marriott for the weekend. Why?"

"So am I. Why don't we meet in the lounge for a nightcap?"

Tina smiled. "That sounds good to me."

The cart arrived and Tina and a couple got on and it headed down the driveway. As Lorenzo got into his car, he looked up and saw Rudy and Patricia on the front porch. They both gave him a big smile and he waved to them. So far, this reunion was going just fine.

Chapter 12

Midnight

A four-piece band and female vocalist were performing when Lorenzo walked into the hotel lounge. He'd talked to Phillip during the drive from Rudy and Patricia's; he was as surprised as Lorenzo was to find out that Josh had blocked Sylvia from talking to him in 2010. They both agreed to keep that information "in the holster" until they needed an extra weapon to use. He'd also reached out to Lee Fleming and worked out a deal where in exchange for Fleming sitting on the story for now, Lorenzo would give him an exclusive interview when he'd made his decision. He looked around and finally spotted Tina in a back booth that faced the door. She'd already ordered a drink and as he slid into his seat, he told the waitress to bring him a double Hennessey while taking note of the singer. There was a soft glow in Tina's brown eyes from the candle on the table as she sipped her drink and looked at Lorenzo.

"So, tell me Lorenzo, what's it like running a big-time record company and having beautiful women chasing after you?"

Lorenzo laughed slightly as the waitress put his drink down in front of him. "I wish I had beautiful women chasing after me. And, despite what Rudy may have told you, I don't exactly 'run the company'. I'm just in charge of finding artists and making sure their records get made."

"That sounds like a lot of fun."

Lorenzo sipped his drink. "The music side of my job is pretty cool. It's the other stuff that gets on my nerves."

"Like what?"

"Oh, the inter-office politics and the paperwork. Getting sued by some women's group over some lyrics in a song that we put out. Even worse are the ego-tripping youngsters who get lucky and have a hit song their first time out." Lorenzo shook his head as Tina took another sip of her drink. "When they're trying to get a deal, they're riding in a raggedy-ass car and willing to do anything you ask them to do. Hell, I even had one guy taking the train and bus to the studio to do his album. But, let them get a hit song and boom, they pull up to the building in a new car or SUV with their posse of flunkies and girls. Add in the effect of illegal downloads, a new ownership group in Tokyo that doesn't seem to understand what we do or how we do it and well…"

"I see," Tina said. "Is that what the call earlier tonight was about? One of your artists?"

Lorenzo shook his head. "No, that was my boss. I've been offered another job and he wanted to know if there was any way he can keep me from taking it."

"Is it a good offer?"

"Actually, it's a great offer," Lorenzo smiled as he answered. "They don't get much better in today's job market."

"That all sounds wonderful Lorenzo. But, for a guy who seems to have the world at his feet, you don't sound too happy."

"Don't get me wrong; I'm very happy with the offer. In fact, it's better than my attorney or I expected. It's just that if I take the new job, I'll have to move to New York. Which I don't really want to do."

Tina looked into Lorenzo's eyes. "Why not? New York's a great city from what I hear."

"New York is cool. I just prefer living in LA. But, that's enough about me, what's going on with you these days?"

Tina shook her head and sipped her drink. "Where do I start? Well, I broke up with my boyfriend last year after catching him screwing my best friend who just happened to also be my business partner.

My father's had two heart attacks in six months and his doctor wants him to take it easy. So, I decided to move back home and take over his practice."

"I'm sorry to hear about your dad. I always liked him. As for the cheating boyfriend and best friend...that's pretty messed up."

"Yeah, well, I'd use another word, but that's the 'Skyline' in me," Tina said.

They laughed at her reference to the tough Southeast San Diego neighborhood they'd both grown up in. "You can take the girl out of Skyline, but you can't take the Skyline out of the girl," Lorenzo said.

"You got that right!" Tina exclaimed as they both laughed and clinked their glasses together.

Lorenzo shifted the subject back to her surprise earlier in the evening. "Why did you want your being here a secret? What's that all about?"

"Well, considering how things ended between us...."

"Tina, that was a long time ago."

"I know but, after what I did, I wasn't sure if you ever wanted to see me again. I guess I was afraid that you were still mad at me."

Lorenzo nodded his head before he looked across the table. "I won't lie, I was mad for a while after it happened but I forgave you years ago. I just wish you had told me the whole story back then."

"I was scared Lorenzo. I didn't know what to do. You were on the road and I was just about to start med school. Be honest: were you really ready to be a father back then?"

"Probably not but, were you ready to be a mother and give up on your dream of becoming a doctor?" Lorenzo had no intention of taking all the blame by himself.

"No I wasn't. And that was a big part of my decision to do what I did. But, I wanted to tell you face to face that I've never stopping thinking about what might have happened between us if I'd handled things differently."

Lorenzo sighed. "To tell you the truth, neither have I. But that's in the past and there's nothing either one of us can do to change what happened." He looked at his watch. "I hate to be a party pooper but, me and the fellas are playing golf in the morning and I need to get some sleep."

"I know what you mean. I'm pretty tired myself," Tina said as she yawned. "I've always been amazed that you guys have stayed so tight over the years."

"It's kind of tough with Reese in Atlanta and DeWitt in DC but, we manage to stay in touch with emails and texts. Plus, I'm in Atlanta a lot on business." Lorenzo sighed. "I just wish Ronnie was here this weekend."

Tina shook her head. "My mother sent me the newspaper articles when he died. He sure had a lot of talent. Too bad he wasted it."

"I agree." Lorenzo finished his drink and stood up. "Come on, I'll walk you home."

"Just like the old days."

"Yeah, just like the old days."

They got up from the booth and started walking to the door. As they passed the band, Lorenzo put a $20 bill in the singer's tip glass and said, "You've got a great voice" as he picked up one of their CDs. The singer smiled and thanked him.

❈❂❈

Rudy and Patricia's bathroom was lit only by scented candles. Patricia was already in the sunken tub when Rudy entered the room. He wore a silk robe as he leaned over the tub to kiss Patricia and she pulled him into the water, robe and all. "Ven a mi papi."

❈❂❈

Lorenzo and Tina stood in front of room 625. It was a nervous Lorenzo who spoke first. "Well, I guess this is good night."

"I guess so." Tina sensed Lorenzo's nervousness. "What's wrong?"

Lorenzo looked around before he turned back to her and smiled. "It's like we're sixteen again, standing on the front porch of 1221 South Glovan Street, knowing your dad was peeking out the window."

"I'm impressed," Tina said. "You still remember the address."

Lorenzo smiled. "I remember the phone number too: 555-9343."

"Very good. By the way, my father had his gun with him."

"Glad I didn't know that back then. I would have never kissed you."

Tina laughed. "You were safe. He's a terrible shot."

"So I could have ended up just wounded instead of dead. That's a relief, I guess."

Tina suddenly took his head in her hands and kissed him passionately.

"I'd forgotten how good a kisser you are," Tina said.

"I've never forgotten how you kiss. Are you sitting with anyone at the dinner tomorrow night?" Lorenzo asked.

Tina shook her head.

"How about sitting with me?"

"I'd like that very much." Tina kissed him again. "Good night Lorenzo."

"Good night Tina. Sweet dreams."

As Lorenzo turned and walked towards the elevator, Tina opened the door to her room, went inside, closed the door, kicked off her shoes and fell across the bed where she lay staring at the ceiling.

Oh what a night it had been and the weekend was just getting started Tina thought as she drifted off to sleep.

Chapter 13

Saturday Morning

T he guys were on the putting green at Whispering Pines Country Club, practicing and sipping Starbucks coffee while waiting for their foursome to be called.

"This is a nice place Rudy," DeWitt said. "What's it cost to belong here?"

"A hundred grand to join plus monthly dues of fifteen hundred. But it's been worth every dollar. I make a lot of business contacts here and so does Patricia. Plus, it's good for RJ and Carmella to be exposed to this part of life," Rudy said.

Reese let out a low, long whistle. "I've got a membership at a club because my house is in a golf community, but I don't spend anywhere near that much cheese."

"I hear what you're saying Rudy, but did you see the way some of those white boys were checking us out in the locker room?" DeWitt asked. "They act like we don't belong here."

Rudy cleaned his putter. "Do you guys remember when I used to work here?"

The guys all said yes or nodded their heads and waited for Rudy to continue.

"I was caddying for this lawyer one day. I was around 16, and he asked me what I wanted to do for a living when I grew up. I told him that I wanted to be a lawyer so I could help people. He told me that was good and to call him when I was ready to go to law school. That's the same lawyer I used to work for." Rudy paused before continuing. "Anyway, he told me that I needed to know that I would run into some ignorant people that no matter how much education I had or how good a lawyer I became, they wouldn't accept or like me just because of the color of my skin. But, they'd respect me if they saw green when they looked at me. As in dollars. Lots and lots of dollars." Rudy looked at his friends with a quiet fire in his eyes. "Well, gentlemen, it's over 20 years later and I've got lots and lots of dollars. So, if somebody doesn't like me or my friends playing here, fuck 'em. I belong here."

✖◈✖

New York City

Sylvia Andrews usually spent summer weekends entertaining at her house in the Hamptons, but she'd been out of town for most of the week so she was in her Montclair office catching up on paperwork and a few loose items, chief among them, getting Lorenzo to agree to her job offer. Dressed in a casual blouse, jeans and sandals, her hair pulled back in a ponytail, she went over things with Jeffrey Weinberg.

"Phillip Walker's a pro and he knows this is a great deal for his client," he said. "My guess is that when you meet with Lorenzo next week, he will have already agreed to the contract."

"I know he's got a long history with Josh, but when I looked into Lorenzo's eyes in LA the other night, I could tell that he was very interested." Sylvia took a drink of water and then turned back to Jeffrey. "Push the lawyer to get an answer as soon possible. And this is most important: make sure he understands there won't be a meeting on Thursday without an agreement in principle."

"Got it. Anything else?" Jeffrey asked as he gathered his things.

"Jessica and the girls already at the beach house?"

Jeffrey smiled. "How'd you guess?"

"Because you've been trying to leave ever since you arrived," Sylvia laughed. "Get out of here. I'll see you Monday. Tell Jessica I said thanks for letting me have you this morning."

Jeffrey stood and headed for the door. "I'll do that," he said. "I'll call you if I hear anything from Phillip over the weekend."

✖✖

It was apparent after the first hole that Rudy was the only one of the group who played on a regular basis. It was more like "Rudy and the 2 & 1/2 Stooges Play Golf" as Lorenzo's game wasn't quite as bad as DeWitt's and Reese's. There was one hole where Reese hit three shots into the water before he finally gave up and threw the ball onto the green. He earned a mock ovation from the others and DeWitt said that he's definitely not Tiger Woods. Lorenzo used his phone to read and send several text messages and at one point, Rudy grabbed the phone from Lorenzo and put it in his golf bag. When Lorenzo said, "Hey man, I was using that", Rudy coolly smiled and said, "You'll get it back after we're through playing" and walked away to his ball. DeWitt and Reese just shook their heads in awe. Same old Rudy. Always in charge.

✖✖

Marriott Hotel Gym

Despite the combination of her late night hanging out with Lorenzo and the early hour of the day, Tina wasn't about to miss putting in her hour on the treadmill, especially not after all the alcohol she'd consumed. She had a massage scheduled for after her workout and she was determined to be good and sore so she could get the maximum benefit of it.

Chapter 14

Whispering Pines Country Club

The guys had finished their round and were having lunch on the patio. Lorenzo got his phone back from Rudy and immediately checked for messages. There were a few but none were from Phillip who right now, was the only person he really wanted to hear from.

"Rudy, has this place changed much since you were a caddy?" DeWitt asked as he buttered a slice of bread.

"Yes it has. For instance, there are ten more black members now."

"How many were there then?" Lorenzo asked even though he already knew the answer.

"Ten less than there are now," Rudy said dryly.

They all laughed at Rudy's response.

Reese changed the subject. "I gotta tell you Lorenzo, you are one lucky brotha! When I saw Tina last night, I almost lost it. I mean, she looked good back in the day but dayummm!"

DeWitt laughed as he pointed at Reese. "And that's coming from a man married to a 25 year-old swimsuit model!"

"Good point DeWitt. I hadn't looked at it that way," Rudy said.

Reese turned and looked at Lorenzo with a mischievous look on his face. "Hey, you know DeWitt's a minister. He could marry you two just like that." Reese snapped his fingers. "Right, D?"

"Just like that! Easy peasey." DeWitt snapped his fingers and laughed.

Rudy looked up from his plate, reached into his pocket and pulled out his phone. "I can call Patricia and see if they've taken down the tent yet."

"Y'all trippin'," Lorenzo said. "It's good seeing Tina this weekend but ain't nothing going to happen between us. Those days are over." He picked up his glass of iced tea and drank deeply from it. "Over."

The others at the table exchanged glances that said they really didn't believe Lorenzo, but no one challenged his response.

※◈※

While the guys were out playing golf, Patricia had DeWitt's wife Jacqueline and their kids out to the house. As Patricia and Jacqueline ate and talked, RJ and Carmella and her friend Jennifer played with DeWitt and Jacqueline's kids in the pool. Meanwhile, as the workers dismantled the tent over the tennis court, Tina enjoyed her "spa day" at the hotel.

※◈※

DeWitt and Reese continued their lifelong game of "the dozens" while the guys waited for their food to be served.

"DeWitt, you do know that the object of golf is to take the fewest strokes, right?" Reese asked as he looked over their scorecards.

"Funny Reese, I was just going to ask you the same question," DeWitt responded.

Reese picked up his cell phone and pretended to take a call. "Hello, just a minute. I'll ask him." He turned to DeWitt. "It's Charles Barkley. He wants to know why you stole his golf swing."

Reese and Lorenzo laughed and exchanged fist bumps before Rudy abruptly changed the subject and mood. "Does anybody remember the last time we were all together?"

They all looked at each other before Lorenzo responded in a soft voice. "Ronnie's funeral."

"That's right Chocks," Rudy said. "And do any of you remember what we all agreed to back then?"

No one said anything. Rudy looked around the table and shook his head. "You guys are un-fucking-believable. We said that we'd get together at least once a year and just hang out."

It was DeWitt who broke the awkward silence. "I vaguely seem to remember something like that."

Reese nodded his head in agreement. "Me too. So, why haven't we done it?"

No one seemed to have an answer so Rudy seized the moment to propose that they attend the NCAA men's basketball Final Four in Dallas next year. He said that he knew a guy who can get great tickets and hotel rooms for a reasonable price.

"Just a minute Rudy," DeWitt laughed. "Your idea of a reasonable price and ours may be two different things. Don't forget, I'm just a struggling preacher in DC."

Now it was the others turn to laugh. "I didn't know there was such a thing as a 'struggling preacher' who's on TV every week with his beautiful wife and does revivals in arenas and stadiums all over the country talking about the 'abundant life' and how you can live it," Reese said as he smacked his right hand on his leg for added emphasis.

Lorenzo chimed in. "And has his choir doing CDs. And who wrote a book with that same beautiful wife that got turned into a very successful movie with a soundtrack that went platinum." He looked at Dewitt. "I made the deals so you know I know."

"I'd forgotten all about 'Building the Perfect Love'," Reese said. "Thanks for pointing that one out Chocks."

"You're welcome," Lorenzo said as he smiled at DeWitt.

"I'll have you know that I don't take a salary from the church and the CDs and books and my speaking engagements are run through my own company," Dewitt said. "Plus, I donate half of the royalties from the CDs to the church."

Reese snorted derisively. "You expect me to believe that?"

"I don't know what you do or don't believe, but God is my judge, not you Mr. Maurice Parker Ellis the Third," DeWitt snarled.

Lorenzo laughed. "Wow DeWitt, you got 'The Third' and everything in there. By the way Reese, he's telling the truth about the CD royalties."

"Yeah well, maybe you can fool your church people but..." Reese said.

Dewitt was genuinely angry now. "But what Reese? What are you are trying to say?"

Rudy jumped in and took back control of the conversation. "Much as I hate to interrupt today's episode of the 'DeWitt and Reese Show' by getting back to the original subject, yes the prices are reasonable and if you want to, we can share rooms to save on costs."

DeWitt glared at Reese.

Lorenzo laughed. "Nothing against any of you guys, but I ain't sharing a room with anybody that doesn't come equipped with titties and a pussy. I'm in; just let me know when and how much my share is."

"Me too," Reese chimed in.

They all turned to look at DeWitt for his decision as their food was served.

DeWitt sighed. "I guess I'm outvoted. I'm in."

"Good!" Rudy said as he grabbed DeWitt's right shoulder with his left hand. "I'll call my guy and get the ball rolling. You guys can just reimburse me. Now Reverend, if you would be so kind as to say grace."

DeWitt asked his friends to join hands and bow their heads. "Dear Father God. Please bless my heathen friends, especially the one who wants me to spend my hard-earned money running around the country watching basketball games. And please bless this food that we're about to enjoy and the hands that prepared it. Amen."

"Amen!"

As he cut into his broiled salmon, Reese couldn't resist taking one last shot at his lifelong friend. "DeWitt, you'd be out of business if it wasn't for heathens like us."

Chapter 15

Patricia waved goodbye from the front steps of the house as Jacqueline and her kids pulled away in their rental car. She'd enjoyed getting to know DeWitt's wife a bit, but Patricia was eager to do some work on an upcoming project. She looked at her phone, punched a button and was almost instantly connected to her son Ramon in Austin as she walked back into the house. "Hey son, let's talk about the proposal for Rosita's Restaurants. I was thinking…"

✖❖✖

The guys were eating when Lorenzo asked a question that made everyone stop and think for a moment.

"Do you guys ever wonder why we made it out of the old neighborhood and why some of the guys we grew up with didn't?"

It was Reese who responded first. "You mean like Ronnie?"

"Yeah, like Ronnie," Lorenzo said. "Think about it: Ronnie had more pure athletic talent than the rest of us combined. He was book-smart too. And yet, he ended up on drugs, in jail and finally dead from AIDS. How does something like that happen to a guy like him?"

DeWitt sipped from his cup of coffee. "That's easy, Ronnie didn't have God in his life."

Lorenzo shook his head. "It can't be that simple DeWitt."

"Yes, it really is," DeWitt said emphatically.

Reese seemed a bit skeptical. "Come on, DeWitt. I know you're a preacher and all, but you really believe it's that simple?"

"Reese, it's called faith and you ought to give it a try sometime," DeWitt said.

Lorenzo continued. "Well, something or somebody protected us along the way. We could have screwed up many times along the way; we sure had the opportunity. But we hung in there no matter what the obstacles we had in front of us. Look how things have turned out for Rudy."

Rudy had been sitting back and just listening to his friends.

"Hey man, I'm just a guy who knew what he wanted to do with his life and followed the rules. That's all."

Lorenzo was incredulous. "Followed the rules? You married a divorced woman five years older than you with a kid and you call that following the rules?"

Rudy just shrugged his shoulders. "Things happen in life that you just can't explain. Like DeWitt becoming a preacher."

Everyone but Lorenzo laughed.

"I'm being serious and you guys want to make jokes. Look around this table. DeWitt's got one of the biggest churches on the East Coast and he's on TV all over the country. Reese is about to become a Vice-President at Coca Cola. I'm one of the highest ranking black executives in the music industry and Rudy, well, Rudy's on a whole other level when it comes to making money. And there's got to be an explanation for why we're all very successful, productive people and why the guy who was better at everything than any of us growing up, threw it all away."

They were all quiet with their thoughts for a moment before DeWitt spoke up. "Here's what I think. I think that God used Ronnie and his life as a lesson to us. We saw what happened to him when he went astray and that's why we kept ourselves on the right path over the years."

Lorenzo pointed at Dewitt. "I think the good Reverend Stewart just might have a point."

"It's about the choices that you make that determine where and how you end up in life," Rudy said. "God bless him but, Ronnie made some terrible choices and they cost him his life. That's the way it goes sometimes."

Lorenzo shook his head. "That's too easy. It's more than that."

"You're right Lorenzo," DeWitt said. "Maybe it was our parents. Maybe it was some of the other people we ran into over the years. Look at me. I wasn't a hard-core criminal but we all know I did my fair share of dirt before the Lord got hold of me. He used Reverend Hammond to bring me back to the church when I got out of that youth camp."

Reese chimed in. "It's like when me and Felicia split up. A lot of people, including my parents, were really sweating me about getting divorced and how it was going to affect my kids. I really struggled with that and I even thought about just going ahead and staying together because of them. But, deep in my heart, I knew that it was over between us and I had to leave. You guys stuck with me and now look how things have turned out. I've got a new wife that I'm crazy about, I get to see my kids whenever I want and I don't even refer to Felicia as 'the plaintiff' anymore."

They all laughed at that last comment.

"Speaking of kids, where are Ronnie's these days?" It was DeWitt who asked.

"I got his son a lawyer when he was charged with burglary about six months ago," Rudy said. "He's doing eighteen months in county jail. Rhonda's living in Vegas with her mother and studying hotel management at UNLV."

There was a moment of silence while the guys absorbed the information.

DeWitt turned to Rudy. "Say Rudy, there's something I've always wanted to ask you. If you had it to do all over, would you still marry Patricia? I mean, with her being Mexican, older than you and already having a kid."

Rudy leaned back in his chair and smiled. "Funny you should bring that up D. Somebody else asked me that the other day." He looked at Lorenzo before continuing. "Things are much different now than when we first met and the interracial part is easier to deal with than it used to be. Back then, Patricia was 24, I was 19, Ramon was still a little kid and all we owned were our dreams. Now, I've got the law firm and the development company and she's got her own business." Rudy shrugged his shoulders. "Who knows what would happen if we met today."

Reese laughed loudly. "I can still remember your stepmother tripping. Didn't she accuse Patricia of 'robbing the cradle'?"

"Hell yea!" Lorenzo said. "I could hear the screaming at my house from across the street."

Rudy smiled broadly as he shook his head. "Shirley thought I wasn't going to finish college once I met Patricia and my pops thought that I was too young to be a father to Ramon. And all along, his real problem was that he thought he wasn't ready to be a grandfather. Now he spoils the kids more than we do!"

Everyone laughs again.

"Here's a thought," Lorenzo said. "What would you guys say to our starting a scholarship in Ronnie's memory at King?"

Reese loved the idea and said so. "I think that's a damn good idea Chocks. But, who would it be for?"

"I hate to admit it, but Reese makes a great point," DeWitt said. "I remember when we were in school, it seemed like the people who needed the most help got the least."

Reese nodded his head. "Ain't that the truth."

"That won't happen this time," Lorenzo stated emphatically. "We'll make the rules that says who gets it. Rudy's a lawyer; he can take care of the legal mumbo-jumbo, right?"

"Yes I can and yes I will."

The discussion went on for a few more minutes over coffee and as they were talking, a man came over to their table and said hello to Rudy. It was golf pro Phil Mickelson and Rudy introduced him to everyone. After greeting the guys and shaking hands with all of them, Mickelson asked Rudy about Patricia and the kids. Before departing, he reminded Rudy of their game scheduled for the coming Tuesday and how much he was looking forward to taking some money off of him. As the world famous golfer walked away, Rudy turned to his obviously impressed buddies and winked. Oh yeah, he definitely belonged here.

Chapter 16

Parking lot of the country club

The fellas stood next to Rudy's Bentley as they talked.

"By the way, I'm preaching at Double Rock tomorrow," DeWitt said. "You guys should come and hear me." He looked directly at Reese. "You just might learn a thing or two about faith."

Reese returned DeWitt's stare. "Thanks D, but me and God are on good terms."

Lorenzo and Rudy both said they'd try to make it and said their goodbyes. Reese and DeWitt had ridden together and they walked towards Reese's rental car, arguing as always.

Reese was heated and animated. "Don't argue with me D. It's not even close. Michael Jordan is the greatest basketball player of all time! It's not even a discussion. Michael Jeffrey Jordan is # 1. End of story."

"Magic is the greatest."

Reese stopped, grabbed DeWitt's left arm and held onto it with his right arm as he held up three fingers with his left. "Can Magic say three-peat? Michael can say it not once but, twice. Plus 2 Olympic gold medals. 72 & 10. 'Space Jam'. Cologne. 'Air Jordans'. And he's got six rings. That's one more than Magic has. Even you know 6 is more than 5. Hell, he owns a team. He will always be the greatest ever! Case closed!"

"What does cologne have to do with basketball?" an exasperated DeWitt said as he removed Reese's hand from his arm and continued walking away from him as an amused Lorenzo and Rudy looked on. "Besides, Magic's a co-owner of the Dodgers and they're worth a lot more than Jordan's team," he said over his shoulder.

Lorenzo smiled. "Those two will never change."

"Probably not," Rudy agreed. "And frankly, I hope they never do." He turned to look directly at Lorenzo before he continued. "So, how it'd go with Tina after you left the house last night?"

"Pretty good, actually. We had a couple of drinks and talked until about 2. Her father's been sick and has to slow down so, she's moving back here to take over his practice."

"I'd heard about her father being ill but I didn't know it was that serious."

Lorenzo shrugged. "His doctor said he should retire. Anyway, I walked her to her room, kissed her good-night at the door and went to my room. By the way, I'm still pissed off at you for not telling me that Tina was coming this weekend. That was foul."

"Yeah, it was," Rudy cheerfully agreed. "But that's how she wanted it. So, that's all that happened? Just a kiss at her room door? After all these years?"

Lorenzo was irritated and it showed in his voice. "Yo man, what the hell is that supposed to mean?"

"Calm down. I'm just checking, that's all."

"Yeah, well, put a halt to that crap right now." Lorenzo threw his arms up in the air in frustration. "Damn, why does everyone think I'm trying to screw Tina this weekend?"

Rudy smiled. "Because we know you better than anyone else does?" he said with a wicked tone to his voice.

Now it was Lorenzo's turn to smile. "Maybe that's the way I used to be but it ain't like that anymore. I just want me and Tina to be friends again. That's all. Besides, she's moving back here and I'm probably moving to New York soon." He sighed. "This is just like the old days. Something always kept us apart. If it wasn't one thing, it was the other. Nothing's changed in all these years."

"Look Chocks, I'm not trying to tell you how to run your life or anything like that. I just don't want to see you get hurt again. Take it nice and slow and enjoy the weekend. Let whatever happens with Tina happen and accept it for what it is. Good, bad or whatever."

Lorenzo smiled. "I hear you. You don't have to worry about me and Tina. We've put all that old stuff behind us." He paused. "Well, I know I have."

"Glad to hear that," Rudy said despite his doubts that Lorenzo had really put it all behind him.

✵✵

Rudy and Patricia's kitchen.

It was a little after 2 o'clock and Patricia, dressed in shorts and a black Bebe tank-top, was sitting at the table working on a laptop computer, surrounded by a pile of papers when Rudy walked in and got a beer out of the refrigerator.

"Where are the kids?"

Patricia didn't look up from her work. "My mother picked them up about an hour ago. How'd the game go?"

"Okay I guess. I shot a 75, Chocks managed a 90 and the 'Doofus Brothers', Reese and DeWitt in your program, shot a magnificent 102 and 105 respectively."

Those last numbers got Patricia's full attention and she looked up from her computer. "102 and 105? I can do better than that and I haven't played in a month." She shook her head. "Were they even trying?"

"Sadly, yes they were." Rudy swigged from the beer bottle and gestured at the papers on the table. "What are you working on?"

"It's an ad campaign for a restaurant chain. The presentation is Tuesday morning. I've been working on the PowerPoint."

"How's it looking?"

"Well, the only thing I'm really concerned about is the fee. We've already cut it 10% because we really want this account. I'm just worried that it's still too high for a company their size."

Rudy drank from his beer again and leaned against a counter. "Don't sell yourself cheap baby. I'm sure you're worth much more than you're asking for. Leave it right where it is now. They want the best; they have to pay for it."

"I appreciate your faith in my talents. Ramon said the same thing when I talked to him earlier." Patricia closed her computer, got up and walked over to Rudy and stood in front of him with her arms around him and laid her head on his chest.

Patricia closed her eyes. "What did Lorenzo say about him and Tina last night?"

"Well, according to him, they had a couple of drinks in the bar, talked for a while and then he walked her to her room and said goodnight. Then he went to his room. Alone."

"You believe him?"

"Why would he lie about something like that?"

"Did he tell her he's thinking about taking a job in New York?"

"He didn't say if he did or not but I'd guess that it came up."

"Did Tina tell him that she's moving back to Diego?"

"She did."

"How did he take it?"

Rudy shrugged his shoulders. "You know how Lorenzo is. He's not going to say how he really feels, just like that." Rudy placed the empty beer bottle on the counter and kissed Patricia on the forehead. "I'm going to take a shower and grab a quick nap. Wake me up at 6:00, okay?"

"Okay."

Rudy was just about out of the kitchen when Patricia said his name and he stopped in the doorway and turned around.

"What?"

"Do you think Tina's moving back here could affect Lorenzo's decision about taking the job in New York?"

"I doubt it. According to him, the offer is too good to turn down and the only thing Lorenzo loves more than living in LA is money. And he'll make a lot of money in New York."

"Money isn't everything," Patricia said.

"Said the woman sitting in the kitchen of a 10 million dollar house who's going to ride in a $150,000 Mercedes-Benz tonight," Rudy smirked.

"Qué puedo decir? Mi esposo me mima." ("What can I say? My husband spoils me.")

Rudy smiled. "Sí, mimarte a ti. Pero, eso es porque me consientes demasiado." ("Yes, I do spoil you. But, that's because you spoil me too.")

Chapter 17

Skyline Drive

Lorenzo stood at the gate across the driveway of King High School and thought about the "good old days". He let his mind wander back to their senior year when the baseball team won the city championship after Ronnie hit the game winning home run and he and Rudy scored ahead of him. Man, did they party that night. His reverie was broken by the ringing of his cell phone. When he looked at it, he saw it was a FaceTime call from Bobby Mitchell, Wilshire's biggest artist and one of Lorenzo's first signings at the label. Lorenzo punched up the video feed.

"What's up playboy?" Lorenzo asked cheerfully.

Bobby got straight to the point. "So when were you planning to tell me?" he asked in an all-business tone.

"Tell you what?" Lorenzo said as he tried to figure out how much Bobby did or didn't know.

"Don't play me Lorenzo. We've known each other too long for that. What's up with me hearing that you met with Sylvia Andrews out in LA Thursday night?"

Arnold Robertson's name was the first one that popped into Lorenzo's head. He and Bobby's manager, Ken Wilmot, had been roommates and frat brothers in college.

"I'm waiting for your answer."

"I wanted to wait until I had something definite to tell you," Lorenzo said. "I figured there was no need to worry you about something that may or may not happen."

"So the rumors are true?"

"Let's just say that I'm thinking about making a move, but I haven't decided yet."

Bobby grimaced. "I got to be honest with you Lo. I ain't happy about this at all. Why are you thinking about leaving?"

"It's a long story," Lorenzo replied.

Bobby wasn't giving an inch. "I'm listening."

Lorenzo sighed as he wondered how much he should tell Bobby who apparently knew more than he was letting on. "Well, there have been some changes over the past few months and there's probably more on the way once Wanatabe finishes their review. I think it's going to be a different company than in the past and I'm not sure I like the direction Josh is going to have to take it in. Plus, the other offer is much better than anything Wilshire's put on the table so far and they probably won't or can't match it."

"You think it would make a difference if I talked to Josh directly? After all, I am the label's number one artist."

Lorenzo had to suppress a laugh as he tried to imagine that conversation. "Maybe, maybe not. Frankly, I don't know if it's going to be Josh's call."

Bobby was agitated and he wasn't hiding his feelings at all. "Hold on playa! I can't go on 'maybe, maybe not'. Look, I signed with Wilshire because of you. You said you'd be there for me and we'd make some money and history together. It's been good so far but now, you talking about running off somewhere else while I'm stuck there for two more records just because of some changes that may be coming. What kind of bullshit is that?"

"What can I tell you?" Lorenzo knew what was really bothering Bobby. When he'd renegotiated his contract two years ago, his manager had tried in vain to get a 'key man' clause inserted that would allow Bobby to leave the label if Lorenzo were ever fired or took a job at another company. "These things happen and it just might be time for me to move on. And if I do, I'm going to recommend that 'Money Mike' gets a shot at running A&R. Hell, he did more on your last project than I did anyway."

"True, but I never approved a mix until you'd heard it and gave your input." Bobby looked off to his right and told someone, "Right, give me a minute" before turning back to the camera. "Well, I've got to do sound check so I can give the people of whatever city I'm in tonight a good show. You still coming to New York next week?"

Lorenzo smiled for the first time during the conversation. "I wouldn't miss seeing you at the Barclays Center for anything. By the way, you're in Charlotte tonight."

"Whatever. See you in a few. And holla at Icy for me. I need him there too, but the dude ain't responding to any of my texts." Icy Gee had rapped on *Come Give Me Yo Love,* Bobby's latest hit song.

"I already did. He'll be there for all three shows. And just so you know, I convinced him to do this just for expenses."

Bobby laughed. "See, now that's why I need you on my side. He told me he wanted 10 G's a night just to do one song."

"And now he doesn't," Lorenzo said smugly. "See you in New York."

Lorenzo ended the call and walked back to his car. The word was out, he thought. It was time to make a decision.

Chapter 18

Saturday Evening

There was a banner in the school's colors over the entrance of the hotel that welcomed the King High School Class of 1993 as they arrived for the evening's activities. Lorenzo stood near the entrance to the ballroom holding the event waiting for Tina to arrive. He turned away for a moment to say hello to someone and when he turned back, Tina was walking towards him. The sight of her with her hair in soft curls down to her shoulders, dressed in a shimmering black cocktail dress and 4-inch, open-toe sandals and carrying a matching clutch, brought a smile to his face and an increase in his heartbeat. Damn, he thought to himself, Tina really is beautiful.

Lorenzo reached out and took Tina's right hand in his and bowing just a bit, kissed it lightly. "Good evening Ms. Davis. So glad you could make it this evening."

"Good evening Mr. Taylor. So very good to see you again."

They both laughed at their exaggerated formality. Lorenzo put his right arm out, Tina slid her left one through it and they walked into the ballroom together as heads turned all over the room. Rudy looked to see what the commotion was all about and when he saw it was Lorenzo and Tina, he smiled and told Patricia to look at who's here.

⁂

The room was decorated with a prom theme and it was a well-dressed crowd that was enjoying seeing each other again. The group was all seated at the same table and Reese and DeWitt continued their good-natured bantering throughout dinner. They kept a running commentary going on how their fellow classmates looked after 20 years and when DeWitt's wife reminded him that he's a minister, he responded that Jesus probably played "the dozens with the Disciples". This comment got Reese going on one of his tangents. "So, when Jesus finally got his crew together, that was when he really started making his mark. I mean, yeah, he had a good message and all, but it wasn't until he formed the Disciples and Paul became his hype man, that he started getting the big crowds and doing big things."

DeWitt's wife started to say something but her husband put up his hand. "Don't say anything Jacqueline. You'll just encourage him and make things worse."

Reese was just getting warmed up. "Man, if I could gotten my hands on Jesus and done his marketing!" Reese exclaimed. "You think I can sell Coca-Cola? Chile please! I would have sold Jesus all over the Holy Land. I would have had him so large; no way would they have crucified him!"

Everyone just looked at Reese before Patricia broke the silence. "Dios mío. Eso es lo más estúpido que nunca he escuchado a nadie decir."

"Translation please," Tina said.

Rudy laughed. "She said, 'My God. That's the stupidest thing I've ever heard anyone say.' And actually, it's probably only in Reese's top ten."

"Well, that's what I think and I'm sticking with it," Reese said as everyone laughed.

❊❂❊

The dinner portion of the evening was over and Rudy was speaking to the crowd and thanking them for coming out and supporting the class of 1993. His experience in speaking before large groups was clearly evident as he spoke without any notes. He acknowledged and thanked the members of the reunion committee for their hard work and then asked Lorenzo, Reese and DeWitt to join him onstage as they had an announcement to make. They got up from their seats at the table and made their way to the stage while wondering what Rudy had in mind.

Rudy smiled at his lifelong friends before he spoke. "As most of you know, the four of us standing here, grew up in the same neighborhood and attended school together from elementary through King. In fact, Lorenzo and I lived across the street from each other from kindergarten on. But, there was actually a fifth member of our group, the late Ronnie Phillips."

The crowd applauded at the mention of Ronnie's name before a loud male voice pierced the air.

"Hell, Ronnie ain't late! He's dead!"

Rudy ignored the voice and continued on as Lorenzo and the other guys looked out into the audience and tried to see who had spoken. "I'm sure everyone here tonight remembers what a great athlete Ronnie was and the records he set at King. To honor his memory, we'd like to announce this evening that starting with next year's graduating class, we'll be awarding a scholarship named for our old friend, Ronnie Leroy Phillips."

The audience was on its feet now, applauding and cheering. "Ronnie! Ronnie! Ronnie!"

"Ronnie Phillips wasn't shit and I ain't giving you a dime!" the voice shouted again when the cheering died down.

Now Rudy was mad and he called the speaker out as he looked out into the audience. "Why don't you show your face since you've got so much to say?"

Finally, through the crowd, a thin figure approached the stage. It was Andrew Parker, Ronnie's chief athletic rival since their days at O'Malley Junior High.

"I said it and I'll say it again! Ronnie Phillips was a washed-up, has-been, good for nothing drug addict who got exactly what he deserved!" Andrew shouted.

All of the fellas were mad but Lorenzo was particularly incensed and had to be restrained from going out into the crowd. Andrew wasn't through.

"You punk-ass bitches from Division Heights wasn't shit in '93 and you ain't shit now!"

The crowd was silent but Lorenzo wasn't. "Why don't you come up here and say that to my face, you punk-ass muthafucka!"

"I ain't here to fight nobody," Andrew said with his hands up in the air. "I'm just saying what nobody else has the guts to say." Andrew looked around at his former classmates. "Why honor somebody like Ronnie? Okay, okay, I give him his props for being a big-time high school hero and all that shit. But when he died from AIDS, he was just another has-been who never amounted to anything after his high school glory days. What's so fucking special about that?"

It was Rudy who responded. "We're honoring Ronnie for what he was to us: a friend. That's what this is all about Andrew. Friendship, honor, loyalty. Things you knew nothing about when we were kids and obviously still don't understand."

Andrew laughed and looked around at the stunned audience. "Give us a fuckin' break. The guy was a loser."

"Only God himself can judge any of us," DeWitt said. "I'm pretty sure that there's none of us who've led a perfect life. Not even you Andrew."

Andrew laughed sardonically. "Oh great. Now the preacher's going to give us a sermon. You taking up a collection too DeWitt?"

Now it DeWitt who was outraged and had to be restrained. "Maybe you do need your ass kicked!"

Rudy decided that he'd heard enough and took back control of the situation as the audience buzzed.

"All right! That's enough! Andrew, you were jealous of Ronnie when we were kids and I can see that things haven't changed one bit in 20 years." Rudy shook his head. "You won man. Ronnie's dead and you're still here. Now, before I change my mind and let Lorenzo come down off this stage, go sit down and shut your mouth."

The crowd applauded again as a chastened Andrew turned and went back to his table and Rudy turned to the crowd.

"I want to apologize to everyone for this, uh, interruption. I'm sure that anyone who wants to contribute to the Ronnie Phillips Scholarship Fund will do so out of the goodness of their hearts and because of their memories of Ronnie and what he meant to all of us. We'll be emailing all of you with information in a few weeks. And with that, it's party time!"

As Rudy and the rest of the fellas walked off the stage, the DJ cranked up Dr. Dre's "Ain't Nothing Like A G Thang" and got the party started.

Chapter 19

Two Hours Later

L orenzo and Tina sat at the table, catching their breath when Reese came over to them. "So, are you two going to sit on your butts the whole party?"

"We've been dancing all night," Tina said.

Lorenzo nodded his head. "Yeah man, we're just taking a short break to catch our breath."

"Well, I see Cassandra Washington standing there all alone and I think she needs a dance partner," Reese said as he drank some water.

Lorenzo laughed. "Remember you're a married man again."

"Remember? How can I forget? I pay the new wife's bills while I'm writing the old one's alimony and child support checks every month." Reese stopped and looked at Lorenzo and Tina. "You two look good together," he said before walking away.

Lorenzo and Tina both smiled as Rudy and Patricia came back and sat down at the table. DeWitt and his wife had already left because he had to preach at 8 o'clock in the morning. Lorenzo poured everyone a glass of champagne and proposed a toast.

"To Patricia and Rudolph Patterson, I wish you everlasting love and happiness, a life filled with love and respect and most of all that God continues to bless you both with his amazing grace."

"Here, here," Tina added.

Patricia kissed Rudy after they'd all sipped their champagne.

"And I want to toast Tina and Lorenzo, two old friends who seem to have found one another again after all these years. Amor es bueno."

"Si, es muy bueno," Rudy said as Lorenzo smiled.

Tina looked around the table. "I guess I'm the only one here who doesn't speak Spanish."

Lorenzo translated this time. "Patricia said 'love is good' and Rudy said, 'Yes, it's very good.'"

Rudy looked at Tina. "I don't know what your father's patient list looks like, but these days, it really pays to speak Spanish in this city."

Patricia nodded her head as did Lorenzo his. "Don't worry Tina," Patricia said. "I've got a client who owns a language academy. He'll have you speaking Espanol in no time at all."

"I'm all for it," Tina said as she shook her head. "Lot of good it did me taking French in high school."

Rudy looked at Lorenzo and Tina. "So, are you two having a good time?"

Tina responded first. "Yes we are. It's a great evening Rudy. You should be very proud of yourself."

"Yeah Mr. Patterson, you did a great job with the dinner," Lorenzo added.

"Thanks but I just wish that crap with Andrew hadn't happened." Rudy shook his head.

"That wasn't your fault baby," Patricia said. "Who knew that fool would start some mess tonight? Let it go."

"Patricia's right Rudy," Tina said. "Andrew was crazy when we were kids and as he showed tonight, he still is."

"I wish you had let me bust him in the mouth just once," Lorenzo said with regret in his voice.

"And exactly what would that have accomplished?" Rudy asked.

Lorenzo looked at his friend. "Maybe not a damn thing, but at least I'd feel a whole lot better right now."

❈❈❈

Lorenzo was headed to the restroom when he bumped into Jeffrey Howard in the hallway.

"What's up Jeff? How are you and Kim doing these days?"

"I'm alright but I can't speak on Kim. Me and her got divorced a couple of years ago."

"I didn't know that. Sorry things didn't work out for you guys. You still living here in Diego?"

"Yeah. After the divorce, I couldn't afford a place of my own so I moved back in with my folks."

Lorenzo grimaced. "Really sorry to hear that. That's got to be rough."

"Oh, it's not so bad. Pops ain't home that much and Moms is still a hell of a cook."

"Well, I'm sure things will get better for you soon," Lorenzo said.

"Frankly, I'm just waiting for them to die so I can have the house to myself."

Lorenzo was obviously taken aback. "I see. Well, at least you've got a plan."

Jeffrey jabbed Lorenzo in the chest with his right index finger. "Yes I do. Yes I do."

❈❈❈

Lorenzo was washing his hands when Andrew Parker walked into the men's room.

"Well, well, well. If it isn't the high and mighty Lorenzo Taylor." Andrew looked around. "Where's the rest of the gang? I thought you boys from Division Heights did everything together."

Lorenzo was trying to keep his composure, but it was getting harder and harder to do so. He sighed and dried his hands. "What do you want Andrew?"

The air was thick with tension as Lorenzo and Andrew glared at each other.

"Fuck you Chocks and the rest of your boys too."

Lorenzo smiled narrowly and said, "No, fuck you," before he punched Andrew in the mouth. He laughed as he looked down at Andrew lying on the tile floor, rubbing his jaw. Lorenzo leaned down and threw one final verbal jab. "In case you want to sue me, my lawyer is Rudolph Patterson. You might have heard of him."

Lorenzo turned and exited the room. As he walked back to the ballroom, he said to no one in particular, "I was right; I do feel better."

※❀※

It was a little after midnight and Lorenzo, Tina, Rudy and Patricia were in Lorenzo's suite winding down. Both men had taken their suit jackets off and Rudy sat on the living room sofa as Patricia lay next to him with her head in his lap. Tina sat in one of the club chairs while Lorenzo served coffee from room service. He hadn't mentioned his restroom encounter with Andrew.

"This is a nice suite," Patricia said as she looked around the room. "We didn't have this much furniture in our first apartment."

Lorenzo laughed. "Well, you can afford a furniture store now." He put the coffee pot back on the warmer and sat down in a chair across from Tina.

"Hell, you can buy one too when you sign your new contract," Rudy retorted.

"Let's not talk about that tonight," Lorenzo said firmly.

As smooth jazz played softly in the background, Rudy told the story about Reese throwing his golf ball across the water hazard earlier that day and Lorenzo told them of his encounter with Jeffrey outside the bathroom. Tina mentioned that it was good to see Charles and Chris Reid still together after almost twenty years of marriage.

"You guys have been married almost as long," Tina remarked. "I guess you've started thinking about how you want to celebrate your twentieth anniversary."

Patricia sat up and shook her head. "Not really. It's still two years away. I just want something simple and elegant at the club for our family and close friends."

"I wonder how much that's gonna cost me," Rudy laughed as he looked at his watch. "We're going to get going. If you two don't have any plans tomorrow, why don't you stop by the house for brunch?"

Lorenzo looked over at Tina. "That sounds good to me."

"Me too," Tina said.

Patricia looked at her husband. "You're cooking, right?"

"Yes, I'm cooking."

Patricia laughed. "Mi tres." ("Me three.")

"Good. Let's say around 11." Rudy stood, stretched and put on his suit jacket. "Come on Patricia, let's give these two their privacy."

Chapter 20

Lorenzo and Tina were finally alone in the suite. They were sitting on the love seat with Tina's head on his shoulder.

"San Diego's changed a lot since we graduated," Lorenzo said. "Do you think you'll be happy living here again?'

"Well, I'm not happy in Hawaii anymore, that's for sure. Plus, I want to be around my folks again, especially my father. That's very important to me right now."

There's a moment of quiet before Tina spoke again.

"What's on your mind right now Lorenzo?"

"Just how comfortable it is being here with you like this. What about you?"

Tina smiled. "Believe it or not, I was thinking about when you had your band."

"Bayside," Lorenzo said reflectively. "Man, I haven't thought about those guys in a while."

"Do you ever see any of them?"

Lorenzo shook his head. "Things didn't end so well for us, so nobody's really kept in touch."

Tina raised her head and looked at Lorenzo. "That's too bad. You guys were really good."

"Yes we were. But, there's still a lot of bitterness from when we broke up. TV One tried to get us to do 'Unsung' a few years ago, but Donnie didn't want to do it if I was involved. So…"

"Do you ever miss playing guitar?" Tina asked. "Or being in a band?"

"I still play every now and then just to keep my chops up. I even played on a couple of records last year. But, no, I don't really miss being in a band or being out on the road for months at a time. I like what I do and I'm pretty good at my job."

Tina hesitated before continuing. "I wonder what would have happened between us if you hadn't been on the road when I found out I was pregnant."

"Tina, there's nothing we can do about that now, so why bring it up again?"

"Maybe I…"

"Let it go," Lorenzo said firmly.

Tina went on. "I was so lonely that summer. You were gone; my sister had just gotten married and moved away. I didn't have anyone to talk to."

"Hey, that's in the past," Lorenzo said firmly. "Stop beating yourself up about it. It's over. There's nothing we can do about it now."

"Haven't you ever wondered why I never got married?"

Lorenzo shook his head. "I never really gave it that much thought. I just figured you hadn't met the right guy yet. Just like I haven't met the right woman."

"You were my first boyfriend, the first man I ever made love with; my first everything. I've been in love with you since I was sixteen years old." Tina paused. "I have never, ever stopped loving you and I probably never will."

Lorenzo stood, leaned down, picked Tina up in his arms and carried her into the bedroom.

❈

Patricia stood on the staircase in the entry hall of their house as Rudy walked up behind her. As he lifted her hair and kissed the back of her neck, she ground her luscious hips into him and moaned.

"Dime la contraseña secreta y usted me puede tener cualquier forma que desee," Patricia whispered. ("Tell me the secret password and you can have me any way you want.")

"Mi nombre es Rudy." ("My name is Rudy.")

"Close enough. Now take me to bed and give me what I need."

"Si senora."

※❂※

The lights of the San Diego skyline twinkled through the windows of the bedroom as Lorenzo and Tina kissed passionately. Lorenzo unzipped her dress and she stepped out of it. He unsnapped her bra and laid her on the bed. He leaned over her and they kissed again. Then, as he removed his clothing, Tina slid her thong panties down her legs and kicked them onto the floor. She lay there watching him undress as the moistness between her thighs increased and tears of anticipation and joy streamed down her cheeks. Neither one of them had spoken since they'd entered the room. There were no words needed for this moment, one that unbeknownst to the other, each had been dreaming about for years, albeit for vastly different reasons.

Lorenzo made love to Tina with a barely controlled animalistic passion and force. His tongue moved with snakelike movements between her legs. Tina moaned and wept with increasing intensity as his tongue continued probing deeper and deeper and his hands kneaded her heaving breasts. He buried his face in the furnace-like heat of her thighs and pinched her firm nipples until she screamed with raw pleasure and squeezed her legs around his head.

When Lorenzo finally came up gasping for air, Tina sat up and lay atop him in the 69 position they'd both loved in the past. As he continued making love to her, she took his rock-hard manhood into her hot, hungry mouth and proceeded to ravish each and every inch. "Oh fuck," Lorenzo groaned as she deep throated him. "You still know how to suck me just right." He laid back and she moved over his erectness and proceeded to ride him as if her life depended on it. She leaned forward so her swinging breasts were within reach of his mouth and tongue as his hips gripped her hips as he eased in and out of her.

Tina moaned with the satisfaction of a woman who hadn't been with a man for over a year. Her pent-up sexual energy had been unleashed and Lorenzo was the beneficiary of her renewed sexuality. She bucked her hips to meet his every thrust and raked her nails across his glistening chest and sensitive, turgid nipples. Tina leaned over and hungrily kissed Lorenzo on the mouth before biting his nipples. This had driven him mad in the past and it still did. He responded by pushing her off him and ordering her to "get on your knees baby." Tina turned to face the head of the bed and got on her hands and knees. Doggy was her favorite position and she arched her back in eager anticipation as Lorenzo came up behind her and thrust into her in one sudden move.

She screamed with pleasure as he pounded her roughly with renewed energy.

In and out.

"You like it rough like this, don't you?" Lorenzo demanded as he smacked Tina's right ass cheek with his open palm.

"You know I love it when you fuck me like this!" Tina screamed. "Do it harder baby!"

In and out. Over and over again.

Chapter 21

Sunday morning

The forecast was for a hot day in San Diego and the sun came up in a blaze of glory. Lorenzo and Tina had made love three times and they were both exhausted when they finally fell into a deep sleep, wrapped in each other's arms. They were still asleep when the phone on the night stand rang. Lorenzo looked at the clock radio and wondered who would be calling him at 7am on a Sunday morning. He sat up on the side of the bed, picked up the phone and spoke quietly so he wouldn't wake up Tina. "Hello."

A female voice on the other end responded. "Good morning Mr. Taylor, this is your wake-up call."

"Wake-up call?" Lorenzo yawned. "I didn't request a wake-up call."

"Would you like to order from room service this morning?"

"No thanks. Wait a minute. On second thought, change that to a pot of coffee and a pitcher of orange juice. And a LA Times if you've got it."

"Will that be all, Mr. Taylor?"

"That's it. Thanks." Lorenzo hung up the phone, turned and nudged a still sleeping Tina. "Wake up sleepy head."

Tina opened her eyes and looked at him. She was still groggy. "Good morning."

"Good morning yourself."

"What time is it?"

"7 o'clock."

Tina groaned. "What are you doing up so early?"

"Somebody left me a wake-up call."

"Who would do something that cruel?"

Lorenzo laughed. "My guess is the Reverend DeWitt Milton Stewart. He's preaching at Double Rock this morning and he made all of us promise to attend."

"Are you going?" Tina yawned.

"Yeah, I guess I'd better," Lorenzo said as he got up from the bed. "I don't want to risk the wrath of DeWitt later on. Besides, he can really preach. Haven't you seen him on TV?"

"I don't watch much religious television."

"You don't know what you're missing. DeWitt can really rock a church."

Tina shook her head in amazement. "That's hard to believe. I mean, he wasn't exactly the preacher type when we were kids as I recall. Didn't he do some time at a youth camp back in 10th grade?"

"Funny you should mention that," Lorenzo said. "People change. We were talking about it just yesterday." He walked towards the bathroom. "I'm going to take a shower. I ordered some coffee and juice from room service. Sign DeWitt's name to the check and add a big tip. That'll teach him to leave me a 7am wake-up call."

Tina laughed. "Okay. I will." Tina looked around the room and caught a glimpse of herself in the mirror. She ran her hands through her hair and sighed. She hadn't felt this good in a long, long time.

※※※

Tina sat on the couch wearing a hotel robe and reading the newspaper when Lorenzo walked in wearing his suit pants and dress shirt and tie.

"The coffee and juice are here."

"Thanks." Lorenzo picked up the phone and punched the operator. "Give me Maurice Ellis' room please." He waited a moment to be connected. "Reese, this is Chocks. Did you get a wake-up call this morning?" He listened and then laughed. "That's exactly what I thought too. Are you going?" He listened again. "You really shouldn't make those kinds of threats against a man of God." He hung up the phone and turned to Tina who had a quizzical look on her face.

"What was all that about?"

"That Reese is a fool," Lorenzo laughed. "He said his phone rang at 7 just like mine and once he heard it was a wake-up call, he tried to pull the phone out of the wall." Lorenzo poured himself a cup of coffee and sat down next to Tina.

"When are you going back to Los Angeles?" she asked.

"This afternoon."

The disappointment was obvious on Tina's face.

Lorenzo sipped his coffee. "What's wrong?" he asked.

"Nothing's wrong. I was just hoping that you were staying longer so we could spend some more time together. That's all."

"I wish I could but I've got business in LA that I have to take care of."

"I understand," Tina said as she stood and stretched. "I'm going to get dressed."

Lorenzo looked at her. "You don't want to shower?" he asked.

"I'll shower when I get to my room."

✖✖

Rudy and Patricia were still in bed. Rudy was laying on his back and Patricia had her head on his chest.

"Come on Rudy, call Lorenzo. I want to know what happened last night and so do you."

"You want to know what happened so bad, **you** call him."

"Just call and tell him that we're not going to be at church to hear DeWitt preach. Tell him that we just woke up."

"Well, at least it's the truth." Rudy reached for the phone on the nightstand beside him. "But, if he gets even a little bit suspicious, I'm handing this phone to you."

✖✖

Lorenzo and Tina walked out of his suite and just as Lorenzo closed the door behind him, the phone inside the room began to ring.

❈❂❈

"There's no answer," Rudy said. "He must have already left for church."

"Try his cell phone."

Rudy looked at Patricia. "No. I'm not going to do that. You'll just have to wait until later to find if they did anything. Not that it's any of your business."

"Well, I hope Tina got herself some loving last night."

"Why the sudden interest in Tina's sex life?" Rudy asked with a puzzled look on his face.

"She said that she hasn't had one since she and her boyfriend split up last year. I can't imagine going without sex that long."

Rudy laughed. "Is that right?"

Patricia rolled over, sat on top of her husband and arched her back. "That's right. Cause baby, I've got a lot more to give you before my mother brings the kids back this afternoon."

"So give me some now," Rudy said as he grabbed her hips.

Patricia kissed her husband on his lips and started working her tongue down his body. It would be a while before they went downstairs.

Chapter 22

Double Rock Baptist Church.

Lorenzo arrived at the church around 8:30 and the choir was singing as he walked into the sanctuary and found a seat. Double Rock was a mid-sized church with a membership of around fifteen hundred. It was one of the oldest and most-well known black churches in the city and its pastor, the Reverend Sylvester Hammond, was an influential force in religious circles and local politics. His wife, Ella, was a traditional 'First Lady', known for her St. John suits and matching hats, shoes and purses.

DeWitt, who usually wore a suit when he preached at his own church, was seated in the pulpit dressed in his ministerial robe. As Lorenzo sat down, he caught DeWitt's eye. DeWitt nodded and smiled. He knew that of all the fellas, he could count on Lorenzo being there. Reverend Hammond, the church's long-time pastor, rose and walked to the podium to introduce DeWitt.

"Our speaker this morning really doesn't need an introduction to many of you. He was raised right here in this sanctuary. As a boy, he served on the Youth Usher Board and sang in the choir. His parents are still faithful members and in fact, we still consider him to be a member of the Double Rock family as well."

Shouts of "Amen" and "Praise The Lord" filled the air as Jacqueline and their kids, along with DeWitt's parents, looked on with pride from the front pew.

Reverend Hammond continued. "So, church family, it is my deep honor and pleasure to introduce to you this morning, a dedicated young man of God, a son of Double Rock Baptist Church, a preacher and pastor of great faith and dedication, the Reverend DeWitt M. Stewart of the Abundant Life Church of Washington, DC."

DeWitt rose from his seat and walked to Reverend Hammond and hugged him tightly as the congregation stood and applauded. It was always humbling to hear the man he considered to be his spiritual father praise him. And even though he'd preached from this pulpit several times before, it was always a thrill to stand there again. He disengaged from Reverend Hammond and made his way to the podium where he placed his Bible, the folder with his printed text and a folded white handkerchief on the raised platform. He bowed his head for a moment, prayed a silent prayer and then looked out into the church before he turned to look at a beaming Reverend Hammond.

"Thank you for that wonderful and very flattering introduction Reverend Hammond. I just hope that I can live up to your very kind words." DeWitt turned back to the congregation. "Reverend Hammond, my fellow brothers and sisters in Christ here on the pulpit, my lovely wife Jacqueline, my children, David, Nathan and Carolyn, my parents Oscar and Lenora Stewart and members of Double Rock, it is indeed an honor and privilege to once again stand before you in the house of the Lord. Let us pray. Father God…"

❈❈

After the service, Lorenzo was the last one in the line to greet DeWitt and his wife, along with Reverend Hammond and his wife at the door of the church. He kissed Jacqueline on her cheek before hugging DeWitt who introduced him to the Hammonds.

"It's good to meet you Mr. Taylor," Reverend Hammond said. "I'm so happy you could worship with us this morning."

"It was my pleasure sir. I've heard so much about you and Mrs. Hammond from DeWitt over the years."

"As have we about you." Reverend Hammond turned to Dewitt. "We'll be upstairs. The ladies have a light breakfast waiting for us."

"I'll be right up as soon as I speak with Lorenzo."

Reverend Hammond and his wife turned and left.

"Reverend Stewart, my brother."

"I knew I could count on you Chocks."

"I wouldn't have missed you preaching for anything. In fact, I woke up at 7 just to make sure I got here in time," Lorenzo said.

They both laughed at that statement.

"Well, I'm glad that you did," DeWitt said with a big smile.

Lorenzo smiled and turned to Jacqueline. "It was good seeing you again Jacqueline. You are more beautiful each time."

She smiled. "It was nice seeing you again too Lorenzo. After this trip, I see why DeWitt's always talking about 'the fellas' and San Diego."

DeWitt took Lorenzo's right arm with his left hand. "Let me talk to you in private." They excused themselves and stepped away from Jacqueline.

"I'm really glad you made it this morning," DeWitt said. "I want to speak with you about something."

"What's that?"

DeWitt hesitated a moment before he spoke. "Well, I don't want to appear selfish, but if you leave Wilshire, where does that leave my deal?"

Lorenzo smiled. "I knew there was something I'd forgot to mention." He looked at his friend. "Not a problem. Your deal is on a project-by-project basis and all Wilshire has is 'first-right-of-refusal' rights. You can go out and get another offer and they can either match it or say no. And if they say no, you know I'll take care of you wherever I am."

"That's a relief off my mind," DeWitt said. "I thought about it last night when I was going over my sermon notes. It just popped into my head from out of nowhere."

Lorenzo laughed. "I thought you were going to tell me you were sick or something."

"No, I'm fine," DeWitt said. "But, there is one other thing. Look, I know you're going through some things right now and I just want you to know that I'm praying for you."

"Well D, I hope you've put in a special request for me 'cause I can use all the help I can get right about now."

DeWitt smiled. "The Lord moves in mysterious ways. Just put things in his hands and you'll be fine. You know you can always call me if you just need someone to talk to." He paused. "By the way, you and Tina sure looked good together this weekend."

"That's what everybody keeps saying."

"It's the truth," DeWitt said. "You guys always looked good together. But, here's the thing Chocks; it takes more than just looking good together to make a relationship work. You have to ask yourself deep down inside this one question: what do 'I' really want?"

Lorenzo smiled ruefully. "That's the problem D. I'm not really sure what I want right now." He looked directly at DeWitt. "So preacher man, got any advice for your old friend?"

DeWitt reached out and put his right hand on Lorenzo's left shoulder. "Trust in God and listen to your heart Lorenzo. Have some faith in yourself. That's my advice to you."

The two old friends embraced before DeWitt and Jacqueline turned to walk back inside the church. "I'll see you in Dallas next year if not before then."

Lorenzo nodded. "You got it."

He turned and walked down the steps of the church with DeWitt's words swirling through his head. "Listen to your heart Lorenzo."

Chapter 23

Rudy and Patricia's House

Rudy was using the outdoor kitchen on the patio to prepare brunch and Lorenzo was sitting on a chair, sipping from a glass of water and watching him cook.

"So, what's going on between you and Tina?"

Lorenzo shrugged. "I'm not sure. We spent the night together and had a long talk about our feelings for each other and what happened in the past."

"And?"

"And she said she still loves me and probably always will."

Rudy stopped what he was doing and turned to look at Lorenzo. "Really? How'd that make you feel?"

"I must admit, it felt pretty good," Lorenzo said with a slight smile on his face.

"Even after, you know…"

"Yeah, even after that and after all these years. But, now she's moving back here just when it looks like I'm moving to New York. Plus, even though I still love her, I'm not 'in love' with her anymore." Lorenzo shook his head. "I guess it's just not meant for us to be together."

"So, you've definitely decided to take the offer and move to New York?"

"Pretty much," Lorenzo said. "I've got a few things to discuss with my lawyer tomorrow but, I'm probably going to accept the offer from

Montclair. Jobs like this don't come around every day." Lorenzo leaned back in his chair and stretched out his legs. "It's probably the best thing. Enjoy this weekend for what it's worth and just move on with our lives."

"Why are you giving up so easy? Maybe there's a way to work things out between the two of you. LA's not so far away from San Diego that you can't see each other when you're out here," Rudy said.

Lorenzo raised his eyebrows. "That's easy for you to say. You don't have any idea what it's like to be single. You and Patricia have been together for a long, long time and neither one of you is going anywhere. Besides, I hate long-distance relationships. They never work out except in the movies."

Rudy slid a pan of chicken enchiladas into the oven, turned down the flame under a pot on the stove and sat down across from Lorenzo.

"You know, there's no guarantee that Patricia and I will be together forever."

"What the hell is that supposed to mean? Are you guys having trouble?"

Rudy sipped from a Bloody Mary. "No, everything is cool." He paused before continuing. "But, it hasn't always been that way. We've had our problems in the past."

"What kinds of problems?"

Rudy looked away for a minute before he continued. "I never told you about it because we worked everything out. But, we almost broke up a few years ago."

"What the hell are you talking about?" Lorenzo asked incredulously.

"Do you remember when Patricia miscarried about 5, 6 years ago?"

Lorenzo's voice was barely audible. "Of course I remember."

"Well, I was working on a big deal around the same time. The other lawyer was a real pretty lady and one thing led to another and well..."

"Well what?" Lorenzo said.

"I had an affair."

Lorenzo shook his head in disbelief. "You had an affair? You cheated on Patricia?"

"Yeah," Rudy said quietly. "And it's something I've regretted every day of my life since."

"How come, I mean, why didn't you ever tell me about this before now?" Lorenzo asked with obvious disappointment in his voice. "I can't believe you're just now telling me after all these years."

"We decided not to tell anyone about it. We didn't want to upset everyone with that kind of news unless we were really going to break up."

"How did Patricia find out?"

"I came home late one night. This was at the old house. Anyway, when I came in, she was sitting in the living room waiting on me. As soon as I saw her sitting there, I knew something was up." Rudy stood and checked on the pan in the oven and the pot on the stove and then turned to face his friend.

"Go on," Lorenzo said.

"Well, she looked at me real cold like and said, 'I know all about your girlfriend and what you've been doing.' I asked her what she was talking about and that's when she showed me the pictures."

"Pictures?"

Rudy nodded his head. "She'd had her suspicions so she hired a private detective to follow me and that's how she found out."

Lorenzo shook his head. He still was in a bit of a daze at what he was hearing. "What happened after that?"

"I tried to deny it but, pictures don't lie. Well, unless they've been altered but these hadn't been." Rudy smiled slightly. "You know, it's funny but once she showed me the pictures, I stopped trying to lie about it and just accepted the fact that she knew. I guess it's like being an addict; once I admitted I had a problem, it was easier to deal with it."

"And what exactly was your problem?" Lorenzo asked coldly.

"Me mostly. It was my dick that got me in trouble and almost cost me my wife and family."

"And half of your money."

Rudy shrugged. "I wasn't worried about the money. I can always make more money. I was worried about losing my wife and family."

Lorenzo shook his head. "I don't get it Rudy. You've got a great wife, beautiful kids, everything any man could ask for. Why were you fucking around with another woman?"

"I've been with Patricia since I was 19 years old and even though I messed around some before we got married, she's still pretty much the only woman I've been with since then. Anyway, I was working long hours with a very attractive woman, one thing led to another and we both got carried away. I don't know, maybe I was trying to prove something to myself."

"What were you trying to prove?" Lorenzo asked.

"That I could still get some 'strange' if I wanted to I guess. Or something like that."

Lorenzo leaned forward in his chair and bowed his head. It was at least a minute before he raised it and looked at Rudy. "I can't believe I'm sitting here listening to you tell me that you cheated on Patricia. Especially right after she lost your baby."

"Hey man, you act like I planned it," Rudy said defensively. "It just happened. You're out there in the world, surrounded by beautiful, sexy women. You know how things can happen."

"Yeah, but it's not supposed to happen to you. You're Rudolph Patterson, male role model to the rest of us mere mortals. Just like Barack Obama."

Rudy sighed. "Well, it did happen to me. But, I got another chance at happiness and now, maybe you do too."

Chapter 24

Patricia was in the kitchen preparing a salad while talking to Tina. They could both see Lorenzo and Rudy talking out on the patio.

"That looks pretty intense. What do you think they're talking about?" Tina asked.

Patricia glanced out at Lorenzo and Rudy.

"Well, knowing Rudy as well as I do, I'm pretty sure he's asking Lorenzo how things went between the two of you last night." Patricia waited for Tina to respond but she didn't say anything. "Well, how **did** things go last night between you and Lorenzo?"

"We just talked most of the night and got caught up with each other."

Patricia smiled. "I sure hope you two did something other than just talk all night."

"Yeah, we did that too," Tina said with an even bigger smile.

"Did you talk about his job offer in New York?"

"Yes we did." Tina paused before continuing. "You know, it's like there's always been something keeping me and Lorenzo apart. First he and his band went on the road backing up that singer. Then I got accepted to med school in Hawaii and he moved to LA after the tour."

Patricia nodded. "That tour was his big break in the music business."

"I know. And that's why I didn't tell him that I was pregnant. I just went ahead, had the procedure and went off to Hawaii. I never even let him know what had happened until it was all over."

"Look Tina, I'm sure that at the time, you did what you thought was best for the both of you," Patricia said. "And, considering how things have turned out for the both of you over the years, you probably did do the best thing."

"I know, but I never gave Lorenzo the chance to decide. I just went ahead without him knowing anything about it. He says that he's forgiven me but, can anybody really forgive someone for doing what I did?"

"You can only take Lorenzo at his word," Patricia said. "I remember when Rudy and I first got together. My parents, especially my father, were upset that he was black and younger than me and his were really concerned about my being older, divorced and with a child." She sighed. "It was one thing after another for a long time."

"What's kept you guys together all these years?"

"This may sound funny but, at first, it was probably as much about spite as it was about love. We were determined to show everybody that no matter what they thought, we were going to stay together. That and the fact that the man knows how to seriously rock my world," Patricia smiled. "We're no different from any other married couple; we've had our problems over the years but Rudy is the man for me. I knew that the first time he said he loved me and Ramon. And, our parents eventually came around too."

Patricia looked out at Rudy talking to Lorenzo. "When my friends or people who don't know Rudy first meet him, they can't believe that I'm married to such a quiet man. Me with my loud, crazy self!" Patricia paused before she continued. "But, underneath that quiet façade is an incredibly strong, loving man. I'm blessed that the person I love the most in life, loves me back. Like I said, we've had our share of problems over the years but, I can't imagine my life without Rudy." Patricia turned back to face Tina. "I know things don't look that great right now for you and Lorenzo getting together but, believe me when I say that man still cares about you."

"And I'm crazy about him." Tina sighed deeply. "But I'm here and now he's about to move to New York."

※※

Lorenzo and Rudy were still talking out on the patio as Rudy prepared to scramble eggs. "So, what did you and Patricia do to get things worked out?" Lorenzo asked.

"We sat up all that night talking about our relationship and our life. The first thing we decided was that this wasn't going to end our marriage if we could help it."

"And that did it?"

Rudy shook his head. "No. We also got marriage and family counseling from a therapist out in La Jolla. She helped us look at ourselves in an honest and open manner. It got pretty deep."

"Rudy, I've known you since we were five years old. You practically lived at my house after your mother died. I'm closer to you than I am to my own brother. Why didn't you tell me about all of this before today?" Lorenzo sounded absolutely heartbroken.

"You think I ever wanted to tell you that I cheated on Patricia? Come on Chocks, I know how you feel about her and I didn't want to lose your respect. I wasn't proud of what I'd done and frankly, I'm not proud of it today." Rudy stirred the contents of the pot.

"So, why tell me now? What's the point of telling me so many years after the fact?"

Rudy stopped stirring and turned to Lorenzo. "Because, unlike a lot of people, I know what happened between you and Tina wasn't all of your fault and that you've always loved her. I also know a little something about honesty and relationships and how important they both are."

"Oh, so now you're an expert on honesty and relationships," Lorenzo said, sarcasm dripping from his voice.

"Touché. I deserve that one." Rudy shook his head. "No, I'm not an expert. Just a very experienced participant. I admit it; I messed up big-time and it almost cost me my wife and family. But, I got a second chance and now, you've got one with Tina." Rudy took a long look at his wife through the window before he turned back to Lorenzo. "Trust me, there's nothing better in the world than being with the one person in the world who loves you as much as you love them."

Rudy put the whisk on the counter and sat down across from Lorenzo.

"The other night, you asked me if I've ever wondered what my life would be like if I hadn't met Patricia when I did. Well, I don't know what it would be like or even what I'd be doing right now." Rudy spread his arms wide. "But I can tell you this: all the money, this house, the cars, none of it would mean a damn thing to me if Patricia and the kids weren't in my life." Rudy held up his left hand and pointed to his platinum wedding band with his right. "This is the most important thing that I own and Patricia is never sexier than when she's wearing nothing but her wedding ring."

Rudy stood up and walked over to the door leading into the house. Before he entered, he turned and looked at Lorenzo. "Like somebody once said in a movie: 'success is nothing without someone you love to share it with.' You need to keep that in mind before you let Tina walk out of your life again. This could be your last chance with her. **Don't screw it up.**"

Chapter 25

The four friends said grace before they dug into the food. Tina prepared a plate for Lorenzo and handed it to him.

"Some people have really changed," Tina said. "There were a lot of people that I just didn't recognize."

Rudy smiled. "Helen Lacy sure recognized Chocks Friday night. I tried to tell you way back in the sixth grade that she had her eye on you."

"It wasn't her lazy eye I was worried about," Lorenzo said as he shook his head. "It was her big butt that had me concerned."

Rudy got up from the table to get more orange juice out of the refrigerator and put it on the table before he sat back down. "You should have seen the look on your face when she started doing the bump with you. I thought you were going to die."

"So did I. But seriously, this has been an interesting weekend. It's really funny to see how much people have changed since the last reunion." Lorenzo drank some juice before he continued. "Ten years ago, people were still lying about what they were doing and planning to do. Now, it's like they've come to grips with what their lives are and accepted it."

"You mean like Jeffrey Howard?" Rudy said.

Lorenzo nodded his head. "Well, maybe that's an extreme example. But, he seems to accept where he is in the world."

"Life has a way of doing that to you," Patricia said.

Tina smiled tightly. "Ain't that the truth."

⁂

While Patricia and Rudy cleaned up after brunch, Lorenzo and Tina sat in the swings of RJ and Carmella's old play set on the other side of the yard.

"I can't believe they haven't taken this thing down," Lorenzo said. "I bet it hasn't been used in years."

Tina looked at him. "So, have you decided to accept the New York offer?"

"It's the logical thing for me to do," Lorenzo said. "An offer like this doesn't come around every day. Plus, if I don't take it, going back to work at Wilshire could be tricky now that they know I've been looking around."

"I see." Tina looked away for a moment before turning back to Lorenzo. "Let me ask you something else. And I want you to be totally honest with me."

"Go ahead."

Tina swallowed hard. "Do you ever want to get married and have kids?"

Of all the things Lorenzo might have expected Tina to ask him, this was near the bottom of the list. He paused for a moment before he responded.

"I'd be lying if I said I don't think about it sometimes. I look at Rudy and Patricia and their kids and yeah, I get a little jealous every now and then. But, I guess that's not in the cards for me. At least not yet. What about you?"

Tina shook her head. "I blew my chance at motherhood a long time ago. As for getting married…who knows." Tina sighed. "I just wish I had been honest with you all those years ago. Maybe then you wouldn't still be mad at me."

Lorenzo laughed.

"What's so funny?"

"You, that's what," Lorenzo said as he reached for his wallet and took out a small picture that he handed to Tina.

"What's this?"

"Just look at it."

It was the picture of them from their senior prom. A smaller copy of the same one that's in his office.

"I can't believe you still have this picture let alone you're carrying it around in your wallet."

Lorenzo looked at Tina. "I carry you with me wherever I go. I always have. That's probably why I'm not married."

❋❂❋

Rudy, Patricia and Lorenzo were standing on the front steps of the house as Tina stood by her car.

"When are you going to New York?" Rudy asked Lorenzo.

"I'm flying there on Wednesday. I'll meet with the label on Thursday and if everything is cool, sign the contract on Friday."

Rudy nodded his head. "Well, if you need anything, all you have to do is ask. Look, you know that I'm more than just a lawyer and I've got lots and lots of clients and other people who are always looking for things to invest in. Hell, I'll even put up money if you want to start your own company."

"You'd do that for me?" Lorenzo asked, a bit stunned at what he'd just heard.

"You're my best friend, you know the music business; why wouldn't I?"

"I don't know what to say," Lorenzo said. "I really appreciate that."

Patricia hugged and kissed him on the cheek. "You'd better not move to New York without us seeing you," she said.

Rudy shook his lifelong friend's hand. "You'll do the right thing. I know you will. And don't forget what we talked about."

"I won't forget and I won't leave without saying goodbye in person."

❋❂❋

Lorenzo and Tina stood next to her car.

"Well, I guess I'd better hit the road," Lorenzo said.

"Be careful. The freeway might be crowded."

"Don't worry about me, I'll be alright." Lorenzo paused. "You should have told me Tina. We made a baby together," he said. "Didn't you trust me to do the right thing?"

Tina smiled as tears ran down her cheeks. "Lorenzo, I trusted you and I knew that you would do the right thing. That's exactly why I didn't tell you. I didn't want you to have to choose between me and your music."

"You still should have told me," Lorenzo said forcefully. "You owed me that much. You owed us that much."

Tina nodded. "I know. You're right. I should have told you." Tina looked Lorenzo in his eyes. "But like you said last night, that's in the past and that's where we should leave it."

Tina got in her car and started it. She slid down the window and looked at Lorenzo. "It was good seeing you this weekend Lorenzo. Good luck in New York." The window went back up, Tina put her car in gear and drove away. Lorenzo shook his head, got into his car, started it, lowered the top and followed Tina's car down the driveway. It was time for him to go home and prepare for the next chapter in his life.

Chapter 26

Monday Morning

The elevator stopped on the 4rd floor and when the doors slid open, Lorenzo saw Arnold Robertson standing there. It was obvious from his reaction that Lorenzo was the last person Arnold wanted to see this morning.

"I'll take the next one," Arnold said weakly.

Lorenzo smiled sarcastically as the doors slid shut. "You do that."

✖✖

Later that morning, Lorenzo was working at his desk while listening to the latest mix of the song "Money Mike" finished over the weekend when there was a knock on the door and Josh Evans stuck his head in.

"Renee's not at her desk. You got a minute?"

Lorenzo stood up behind his desk and hit Pause on the stereo's remote. "Of course Josh. I've always got time for you. You want something to drink?"

Josh entered the office and sat down on the couch. "No thanks, I'm good." He pointed to one of the speakers on the wall. "Is that Michelle Casey?"

"Yes. 'Money Mike' finished the mix over the weekend. I'm thinking about testing it in a few clubs this weekend," Lorenzo said.

"Sounds good." Josh settled back into the couch. "I was hoping that we could have a chat and see where we are."

123

"No problem at all," Lorenzo said as he walked over to the chair across from the couch and sat down.

"I hear you're going to New York this week."

Lorenzo nodded. "Bobby Mitchell's got three shows at the Barclays Center. Thursday, Friday and Saturday."

"Is that all you're going there for?"

Lorenzo shifted in his seat. "Josh, if you're asking if I'm meeting with Sylvia Andrews while I'm there, the answer is yes."

"I appreciate your honesty even if I don't like your answer." Josh sighed before he continued. "Look Lorenzo, I wish I could match the offer but, my hands are tied right now with this review and everything. I also wish it was anyone but Sylvia and Montclair. They represent everything that's gone wrong with the music business!"

"Well Josh, that's your opinion and I respect it even if I don't agree with it. They're not exactly the 'evil empire' as you portray them."

Josh grimaced. "That's exactly what they are and Sylvia's their empress. She treats her artists and their music like they're widgets or something. 'Product is our lifeblood' is what she said in an interview a while back. That's what she calls music – product."

"Well, I've always been about the music," Lorenzo said forcefully "and that's not going to change wherever I work."

"The only way that won't change is if you stay here or start your own label. Otherwise, you'll just end up becoming another one of Sylvia's foot soldiers."

Lorenzo looked directly at Josh. "Is that why you didn't give her permission to talk to me three years ago before I signed my last contract?"

Josh was surprised by Lorenzo's question. "How did you find out about that?"

"I've got my sources too Josh," Lorenzo smiled.

Josh smiled tightly. "You were still under contract at the time and we had an exclusive negotiation window with you that I had no intention of waiving. You must admit, with the money you got from the sale and all, it worked out okay for you."

"True," Lorenzo said with an edge to his voice. "But Josh, you still should have told me or Phillip that she'd asked to talk with me."

Josh smiled thinly and nodded his head. "You're right. I should have told you or at least had Arnold talk to your lawyer about it. I thought I was looking out for your best interests, but to be honest, I was probably looking out for the best interests of this company." Josh sighed. "Maybe now's the right time for you to spread your wings and leave the nest."

Josh stood and Lorenzo did too. They embraced and Josh turned to leave. Josh stopped at the door, turned and looked around the office. "This place won't be the same without you." Josh smiled as he pointed at a picture on the wall. "We had us some fun didn't we?"

"Yes we did," Lorenzo agreed as he looked at the photo Josh pointed to. "I'll never forget that convention in Miami. I thought your wife was going to kill you over that girl."

Josh laughed and rubbed his left bicep with his right hand. "So did I. Thank God it was just a flesh wound." He paused again. "If you change your mind, give me a call. I'll leave a light on just in case."

"I'll keep that in mind. Thanks for everything Josh." Lorenzo meant every word and Josh knew it. It had been a great run for them.

"No, Lorenzo, thank you for everything. It's been one hell of a ride. I wish you the very best whatever you decide to do," Josh said. "Just make sure you listen to your heart." Josh turned to leave and then stopped. "If it's not too much to ask, on your way out the door, could you make sure the Michelle Casey record is a hit?"

Lorenzo smiled. "I'll do my best to make sure that happens."

"Thanks, I appreciate that." Josh walked out of the office as Lorenzo picked up his guitar and started strumming it idly.

※❈

It was mid-afternoon and Lorenzo was staring out the big window of his office, deep in thought when his contemplation was interrupted by Renee's voice over the intercom. "Phillip's on line one."

Lorenzo walked over to his desk and picked up the phone. "Yeah Phil." He listened and then wrote on a notepad. "I'll see you at the airport. Thanks."

He picked up his cell phone and sent a text message. Where are you?

The response was almost immediate. At the library. Why?

Lorenzo typed back. I need to talk you about something. Have you had lunch yet? I'll bring Yow's.

Make sure you get shrimp fried rice with the large prawns.

Lorenzo smiled as he responded. I'm leaving the office now. See you in about 45 minutes.

Okay. I'll meet you at the tables near the student center.

Lorenzo smiled again as he typed out Thanks. He grabbed his car keys off the desk and left the room. He walked into Renee's office and stopped at her desk. "I'm going out for a while. Do me a favor; call Yow's and order a #16 combo for two. Tell them I'm on the way to pick it up."

"Large prawns?" Renee asked.

"You know it."

Renee smiled to herself. "Will you be back later?"

"I'm not sure. Call me on my cell if you need me."

Renee held up a large white envelope. "This was just delivered. It's from that TV chef, Warren Graham."

"He catered the party Friday night. He's trying to open up a new restaurant and said he'd send over the business plan," Lorenzo said. "Make a copy and send it over to Ira for his review and put the original in my bag. I'll read it on the plane."

"I'll take care of it," Renee said. "Have a good lunch. Say hello for me."

Lorenzo smiled. "I'll do that." He walked out into the hallway and strode with purpose as he headed for the elevators where he pushed the "Down" button and waited for a car to arrive. When it arrived, he stepped in and pushed the button marked P1. Alone with his thoughts, Lorenzo closed his eyes and enjoyed the silent descent to the parking garage.

Chapter 27

Toting a bag full of take-out containers from Yow's Chinese Palace, a jacket-less Lorenzo walked across the USC campus south of downtown. He'd been there just a few weeks ago to speak to a class at the Jimmy Iovine and Andre Young Academy for Arts, Technology & the Business of Innovation so he had a pretty good sense of where he was headed. Still, just to be sure, he flagged down a university security officer and asked for directions. As he walked in the direction that he'd been pointed, he passed various students and university personnel going about their business. His phone chirped and he stopped to read the text message on the screen. diet coke okay with you? He smiled, typed yes and resumed walking.

Lorenzo arrived at the student center where he spotted who he was meeting for lunch. His ex-girlfriend, Uvanda Wilson, was sitting at a four-person table with two bottles of Diet Coke and two cups of ice on it. Her Louis Vuitton tote was on a chair next to her and she was dressed in a white blouse, black flared pants and red suede peep-toe pumps. Her accessories were tasteful and understated and consisted of a sterling silver Tiffany link bracelet and Cartier watch. The flashiest things about her were her luscious figure and Gucci sunglasses. When she looked up from her HTC One phone and saw Lorenzo walking towards her, she stood up to greet him. They hugged like old friends who hadn't seen each other for a while and exchanged a light kiss on the lips.

Lorenzo stepped back and took a long look at Uvanda. "Dayumm girl, I think it's impossible for you not to look good."

"Still got that silver tongue I see," she responded.

"Well, as I recall, somebody used to love my silver tongue when I.."

Uvanda interrupted him. "And she misses it every night."

There was an awkward pause before Lorenzo and then Uvanda laughed. It was Lorenzo who spoke first. "Thanks for taking time to meet," Lorenzo said. "I really appreciate it."

Uvanda laughed. "I can always find time for food from Yow's."

"Oh wow," Lorenzo said trying to act hurt. "So it's like that now huh? It's not me, it's Yow's shrimp fried rice and prawns that you care about."

Uvanda smiled and lightly tapped Lorenzo on his hand. "You know I'm just messing with you man. Now sit down and break out that food."

"By the way, Renee says hello," Lorenzo said.

"You told her we were having lunch?"

Lorenzo shook his head. "No, not in so many words. But I asked her to phone in the order and she asked about the large prawns, and well...one plus one still equals two."

"That woman knows wayyyy too much about your personal business," Uvanda laughed.

"You're probably right, but Lord knows she makes my life a lot easier to manage," Lorenzo said as he took the containers, paper plates, chopsticks and packets of soy sauce and hot mustard out of the bag and Uvanda started putting food on the plates. "So, how's school going?" Lorenzo asked.

"Some of my classes this semester are killing me, but I'm hanging in there."

Lorenzo looked at her and spoke with concern in his voice. "But your grades are good, right?"

"Don't worry," Uvanda said reassuringly. "I'm not wasting your money. I'm going to get my degree on time and I'm going to pay you back every dime." Lorenzo was helping Uvanda with her tuition.

"Oh, I'm not worried about that. I've never had any doubts that you won't get it. That's the least of my worries these days," Lorenzo responded.

Uvanda looked at him directly. "So, what's so important that you drove all the way from Beverly Hills in the middle of the afternoon?" Uvanda knew it had to be something important for Lorenzo to leave his office and come downtown just to have lunch with her.

Lorenzo leaned back in his chair and told her everything that had happened since his meeting with Sylvia. Uvanda ate as she listened, interrupting only twice to ask a question. As he talked, it was clear to her that Lorenzo was torn about the possibility of leaving Wilshire and Los Angeles, but that he also believed he needed a change both professionally and personally. It wasn't easy listening to the man she'd been madly in love with talk about being with another woman just a few days ago, but Uvanda also knew that Lorenzo trusted her judgment and that's why he was pouring his heart out to her at this moment.

"So, that's pretty much it," he said as he wrapped up his story. "I don't really want to leave Wilshire or LA, but I might have to." He picked up his chopsticks and started eating again.

Uvanda took a sip of soda and wiped her mouth with a napkin. She shook her head slightly as she stared across the table at Lorenzo.

"What?" he asked.

Uvanda was matter-of-fact when she answered. "What do you want me to say?"

"I want you to tell me what you think I should do about my problems," Lorenzo said.

Uvanda shook her head again. "You can be a real a-hole at times Lorenzo and this is one of them. You come here, tell me this story about fucking your high-school sweetheart over the weekend, a woman who might I point out, that I'm just hearing about for the first time, and that you have to choose between a job that made you a rich man and one that could make you even richer. And then, you have the nerve to sit there and ask me what I think you should do about your, quote unquote, problems."

Lorenzo stared at her silently.

"You don't have problems Lorenzo. You just have decisions to make." Uvanda gathered her things, stood up and put on her sunglasses. "I've got a study group to get to. Thanks for lunch and good luck in New York." She turned to leave but stopped when Lorenzo grabbed her hand.

"So that's it – good luck in New York?" Lorenzo expected and frankly, needed more from her than just that right now.

Uvanda looked down at Lorenzo who was still seated. "Lorenzo, we've known each other for what, five-six years now, and you've always done what you think other people think you should do. That's one of the reasons we broke up; you were worried what others might think of your girlfriend being a stripper. Well, this time you need to do what Lorenzo wants to do. You want to stay at Wilshire and try and work things out with the woman in San Diego; do it. Or, you can take the job in New York and keep moving forward with your career and life. Do what's going to make you happy. Do what your heart tells you to do. And oh, I hope you used a condom."

"Of course I did. I'm not stupid."

Uvanda turned, walked away and never looked back. Lorenzo sat and watched her fade into the distance as his mind swirled with a dozen different thoughts. Uvanda had said the same thing everyone else had said lately: do what your heart tells you to do. The problem was that Lorenzo didn't have a clue as to what that was.

✳✳✳

Later that night, Lorenzo sat on the terrace outside his bedroom listening to music on his iPad. His swimming pool shimmered beneath him as he sipped Johnny Walker Black Label and smoked one of the Cohiba cigars that Bobby Mitchell had given him on his last birthday. Eric Benet's ballad "I Wanna Be Loved" came on as the lights of nighttime Los Angeles twinkled in the distance. Lorenzo picked up his phone and punched in the numbers. "Hello, Davis residence," a woman said on the other end.

"Hello Mrs. Davis, this is Lorenzo Taylor." He listened. "Yes ma'am, it has been a long time." He listened. "Yes, I'm still fooling around with music." He listened again. "No, I'm still single. Uh, is Tina in?"

Lorenzo waited for Tina to come on the line. "Hello Lorenzo, this is a surprise."

"Tina, we need to talk," Lorenzo said in a matter of fact voice.

It would be four hours before he hung up the phone.

Chapter 28

Wednesday Morning

Tuesday had been a fairly quiet day after Lorenzo and Phillip met with Ira Goldman over breakfast at the Four Seasons Hotel in Beverly Hills to go over a few final details of the Montclair offer before they left for New York City. Ira ran through the tax implications of the proposed deal and suggested that the production end of the deal be funneled through the loan-out company that Lorenzo had used before going to work at Wilshire. He also mentioned that he'd have an analysis of Warren Graham's business plan done as soon as possible. After that, Lorenzo spent the rest of the day in his office dealing with paperwork and other items that required his attention. He and Money Mike finalized plans to test the Michelle Casey single that weekend in 20 clubs around the country. Mike would personally take it to LIV in Miami, one of the hottest clubs in the country, for their regular Sunday night blow-out while Lorenzo worked it in New York. He had another brief meeting with Josh, but it really didn't change anything. They both knew that in all likelihood, these were Lorenzo's final days at Wilshire and there was a sense of shared sadness about that realization. He also replayed parts of the previous night's long phone conversation with Tina in his mind.

They'd covered a lot of old ground during those four hours and both of them had gotten a lot off their respective chests. It was a conversation many years in the making and when it was over, both parties felt that they knew exactly where the other stood.

Lorenzo and Phillip now sat next to each other in the first class cabin of an American Airlines plane as other passengers boarded. Lorenzo looked at photos of the reunion on his iPad while Phillip read a magazine.

"Phil, let me ask you something. If you had to choose between your wife and job right now, which would you choose?"

Phillip glanced at Lorenzo's iPad and then looked at him.

"What kind of question is that?"

"Just answer it."

"My wife of course. But what does that have to do with anything?"

Lorenzo turned to look at his attorney. "How did you know that Sheila was the one for you? Why did you marry her?"

Phillip smiled. "It's kind of funny actually. We had been dating for a few months and she invited me to her church picnic. When the food was ready, she turned to me and asked, 'Do you want me to fix you a plate?' Right then and there, that's when I knew. No other woman had ever offered to fix me a plate before."

Lorenzo flashed back to Sunday when Tina fixed him a plate of food. "And that was it?"

"Of course not," Phillip laughed. "It was also the fact that she had captured my heart. Fixing me a plate of food was just icing on the cake."

Phillip looked at Lorenzo over his reading glasses. "Are you okay?"

"I'm fine," Lorenzo said with a huge smile on his face. "Never been better." He took off his seat belt and stood up.

Phillip was alarmed. "What are you doing?"

"I can't go to New York with you. There's something I have to take care of," Lorenzo said as he put on his suit jacket and grabbed his Louis Vuitton bag.

"Lorenzo, this isn't funny. Now, sit your ass down." A frantic Phillip stood up and tried to block Lorenzo's way. "Please don't do this to me, I mean yourself. This is a great deal. What am I supposed to tell Sylvia and Jeffrey?"

"Tell them I'm catching the red-eye." Lorenzo turned to the flight attendant. "I need to get my carry-on bag please."

"Right away sir," the attendant said.

Lorenzo looked at Phillip. "Keep your phone on. I'll call you later."

A frustrated and confused Phillip slumped in his seat as Lorenzo collected his carry-on bag and exited the plane. He pushed the call button for the attendant. "I need a drink."

❈❈

Lorenzo talked on his phone as he rolled his bag and carry-on case through the crowded terminal. "Hey Josh, this is Lorenzo. If you were serious about helping me start my own label, I've got an idea I want to run by you." He listened. "Okay, here's what I'm thinking…"

❈❈

Thursday Morning

Dressed for class, Uvanda walked into the kitchen of her white two-story Spanish-style duplex on Orange Avenue in the Fairfax District. *Good Morning America* played on the small flat-screen television on the counter and as Uvanda poured herself a cup of coffee, the sound of Michael Jackson's *Remember The Time* wafted through the open window.

"Where's that music coming from?" she wondered to herself.

Uvanda put down her coffee cup, walked through the house and out the front door as the music grew louder and louder. When she reached the steps, she was stunned by the sight and sound that greeted her. There was a digital billboard truck parked in the middle of the street with its speakers blaring the song and on the side of the truck, there was a huge sign that said UVANDA, WILL YOU MARRY ME?

As a speechless Uvanda stood and stared openmouthed at the scene, her neighbors came out of their houses to see what all the fuss was. The driver started the truck and drove away to reveal Lorenzo standing there. Lorenzo walked up to the bottom of the steps where Uvanda stood.

135

"What, what are you doing here? Aren't you supposed to be in New York today?" Uvanda was shocked at his presence in front of her.

Lorenzo smiled. "I'm not going to New York." He reached out and handed a red ring box to her. "This is for you."

"What is it?"

"Open it," Lorenzo said.

Uvanda opened the box to reveal a five-carat marquise solitaire diamond set in a platinum band. She was stunned and her voice was soft when she finally spoke. "What does this mean?"

"It means that I know it's you Uvanda. You're the one for me," Lorenzo said. "I finally figured it out while I was sitting on the plane yesterday. I was on my way to New York to sign a contract for a great job and more money than I ever dreamed about making. It's everything I ever thought I wanted. But, as I sat there thinking about all the changes that were about to happen in my life, I realized that I was listening to all the wrong things."

Uvanda looked at him through her tears. "What were you listening to?"

"I was listening to my ego and wallet instead of my heart," Lorenzo said. "And when I started listening to my heart, that's when I knew what's been missing in my life. You."

"What about New York? Your new job? Your old girlfriend in San Diego?" Uvanda asked.

"I made a deal with Josh last night. I'm going to have my own label with distribution through Wilshire and Rudy's going to help me with the start-up financing. As for Tina, that's over. She's out of my system forever. Last weekend is something that will never happen again. You've got my word on that."

Uvanda wanted to believe Lorenzo but she had to ask. "Are you sure this is what you want?"

"Baby, I've never been surer of anything in my life. Uvanda, I'm ready to love and be loved and I think you are too. And if you are, I'm ready to try and make things work between us." Lorenzo walked up the steps to where she stood and took her hands in his. "I'm here because I like you. I want you. I love you. I want you to be mine and I want to be yours." He paused. "You're the one that has my heart Uvanda."

"You've had mine since the first day we met," she said softly.

"I know that now." Lorenzo got down on one knee. "Uvanda Marie Wilson, will you be my wife?"

Uvanda looked down at him. "You promise to keep it one hundred?"

"Until the day I die," Lorenzo responded.

"Then yes Lorenzo Renaldo Taylor, I will be your wife," Uvanda said through tears of joy.

Uvanda's neighbors burst out with applause and cheers as Lorenzo put the ring on her left hand, then stood up and kissed her deeply and passionately.

"I love you Uvanda."

"I love you Lorenzo."

Epilogue

One Year Later

When he left LAX, Lorenzo called Elaine Jacobson, aka "The Jeweler to the Stars", to purchase Uvanda's engagement ring. Then late into the night, with Phillip on the phone from New York and Rudy from his home and Ira Goldman by his side, he sat in Josh Evans' office and hammered out the deal that gave him his own Wilshire-distributed label. The key to the deal was Josh's personal guarantee and a one million dollar non-recoupable payment to Lorenzo for "personal services" that were purposely left undefined in the contract. It was his way of atoning for not telling Lorenzo that Sylvia Andrews had tried to hire him three years earlier. The negotiations were made much easier by the fact that Josh used his personal attorney and not Arnold Robertson who left the company shortly after Wanatabe's review and reorganization was completed.

Once Sylvia Andrews, who had been absolutely furious when Phillip called Jeffrey Weinberg to say Lorenzo wasn't coming to Montclair, calmed down, she offered to create a head of West Coast Operations position and let him stay in LA. Lorenzo had been tempted, but his personal relationship with Josh was too much for her to overcome. Sylvia hired Lewis Purcell, but word on the street was that she was unhappy with his work and was already looking to replace him.

Lorenzo named his label Taylormade Records and his deal with Wilshire called for him to deliver two albums a year while also serving as a consultant to the label. Per his strong recommendation, "Money Mike" Morrison was promoted to senior director of A&R and with Lorenzo's guidance, he was turning out just fine. Renee left Wilshire to work for Lorenzo as the general manager of the new company.

Lorenzo and Uvanda were married in a private ceremony attended by just a small group of family and friends on the beach in Cabo San Lucas, Mexico during the previous Thanksgiving weekend. She'd graduated with honors from USC the following June and taken a job as a bookkeeper with an accounting firm in Century City. Lorenzo signed two artists, including Dina Jackson, the singer he'd heard in the hotel lounge in San Diego during the reunion, and leased a recording studio in Hollywood which he made his new base of operations. He was there recording Dina's debut album when Renee walked into the control room and said, "Uvanda's here to see you. She says it's important."

"Okay. Tell her I'll be right there."

Renee nodded and exited the room. After telling the engineer the changes he wanted made, Lorenzo walked out into the outer office of the studio where a beaming Uvanda gave him the news he'd been waiting a lifetime to hear.

"We're pregnant!"

Acknowledgments

This book would not exist without the help, love, prayers and support of many people.

First and foremost, I want to thank Almighty God for his amazing grace and love. He has blessed and shown me mercy even when I didn't deserve it and for that, I am eternally grateful and thankful.

I would have never finished this book without my editor and big sister Janice Frazier-Scott and my friend and manager Terry Mitchell Collier. These two incredible women made this possible with their love, hard work, unwavering belief in me, and dedication to excellence. I am forever indebted to you both.

THANK YOUS

To Glenda Amena Tariq and Nathan Freeman – for your prayers, love, support, food, and "projects" that kept me going when times were hard.

To my father Claude E. Freeman – you may not have made me but you always treated and loved me like you did and for that, I am eternally grateful.

To my uncles David S. Cunningham, Jr and Bishop Ronald M. Cunningham – for your unconditional love and being positive role models that I've looked up to for as long as I can remember.

To my "other" family the Austins – it's too many of you to name individually and if I left out one of you, I'd never hear the rest of it so just know that I love each and every one of you very much except for maybe...well okay, her too.

To the best friend a person could ever have – L. Bishop Austin. I hope to someday be half the man and person that you are.

To my friend and writing mentor Steven Ivory – I hope you are even half as proud of me as I am of you. Thank you for encouraging, leading, teaching and supporting me all along the way. And, most importantly, for being right when you told me to "Take your ego out of your writing Charlie."

To Hamilton Cloud and Belma Michael Johnson for giving me a chance on the NAACP Image Awards staff in 1993 which set me out on the journey that has led me to this point.

To Janice Roshalle Littlejohn and Kimberla Lawson Roby for not telling me just how damn hard writing this book was going to be. If you had, I might not have done it.

To Dina Ruth Andrews for being the "Diva" that you are.

To Richard "Big Daddy" Wright for just being who you are and for never forgetting where you came from.

To Rae Patrick for the birthday meals, laughing at my jokes and being a friend just when I needed one the most.

To Reggie Collier, thank you for making it possible for Terry to be a part of my life personally and professionally.

To the teachers, professors and counselors who have inspired and shaped me over the years: Mrs. Mary Weakley Armstrong of Memphis, TN (3rd grade); Dr. Patricia Worthy Oyeshiku and Mr. Dave Wightman of San Diego, CA (high school); Ms. Paulette Bailey, Mr. Roberto Mancia and Mr. Thurman Robinson of Los Angeles, CA (college); Ms. Cynthia L. Clayton (State of California) and Ms. Klaudia Macias (LATTC).

To the baddest rhythm guitarist in the world and my "godfather" in the music industry, Al McKay; to my dear friends Luisa Justiz Dunn and her incredibly talented husband Larry "Dunnomatic" Dunn;

Maurice "Big Memphis" White for sharing your wisdom and music; Tito Jackson, 3T and the late Dolores "Dee Dee" Martes Jackson for the good times on Petit Avenue in Encino; The Phenix Horns, Esq: Rhamlee Michael Davis, Michael Harris, Don Myrick (deceased) and Louis Satterfield (deceased) for letting me work with you during the 1985 Phil Collins world tour; Philip Bailey for making me laugh and for sharing your incredible vocal gifts with the world for over 40 years; Susie and Ralph Johnson for your generosity, big hearts and Ralph's legendary lasagna; Andrew Woolfolk for telling Reese and Art to hire me; Shelly and Verdine White for always keeping it real with me; Richie Salvato for putting up with my nonsense and teaching me "Stage Right and Stage Left"; Lon Rosen for always taking my calls over the years; M.C. Hammer and Louis K. Burrell for letting me be a part of your incredible accomplishments; Jonathan E.D. Moseley, Sr for the years of friendship, support and laughter – they still don't know how "we did it" and made it look so easy; The Horns of Fire: Gary Bias, Ray Brown and Reggie Young for making me look good (I still have the cigar case); Kraig S. Brooks for the chauffeured Jaguar at Heathrow Airport in London; Rodney Saulsberry for the many, many conversations and for accepting the inevitable in the MJ vs Prince argument; Ray "Eagle-Eye" McDonald for the proofreading; Michael "Playmaker" Irvin for letting me be part of your Hall of Fame team in 2007 and to an incredibly talented artist, Jonathan Marcial, for taking my ideas for the cover and turning them into reality.

A very special thank you to the Culver City Crew for helping me save myself one day at a time.

To Jacqueline – after all these years, the sound of your voice still takes my breath away.

Much love and May God bless you always and forevermore,

Charles L. Freeman, Jr

(E-mail: charleslfreemanjr@yahoo.com)

(Twitter: @charleslfreemn)